Are You *Sure* You Want to Turn down FEAR STREET?

The most *horrifying* things seem to happen to those who live on Fear Street.

The town of Shadyside is nice enough. And the students at Shadyside High seem to be an average group of kids.

So why does everyone tell such stories about Fear Street . . . ?

About unspeakable terrors, troubled cries in the night, twisted nightmares . . .

About people who venture into the Fear Street woods and are never seen again . . .

About strange cries late at night from the old Simon Fear mansion—a house that's been deserted for fifty years . . .

About lost teenagers, mysterious fires, brutal crimes, unsolved mysteries . . .

About normal people—people just like *you*—who turn down Fear Street . . . and are never quite normal again!

Go ahead. Take a walk down Fear Street. Those stories couldn't be true. No way. There couldn't be that much terror awaiting you on one narrow, old street—*could* there?

Don't miss these chilling tales from

FEAR STREET®

After hours, the horror continues at

FEAR STREET NIGHTS®

R.L. STINE

FEAR STREET®

THE NEW GIRL

Simon Pulse
New York London Toronto Sydney

A Parachute Press book

SIMON PULSE
An imprint of Simon & Schuster Children's Publishing Division
1230 Avenue of the Americas, New York, NY 10020
Copyright © 1989 by Parachute Press, L.L.C.
All rights reserved, including the right of reproduction in
whole or in part in any form.
SIMON PULSE and colophon are registered trademarks
of Simon & Schuster, Inc.
FEAR STREET is a registered trademark of Parachute Press, Inc.
Designed by Sammy Yuen Jr.
The text of this book was set in Times.
Manufactured in the United States of America
First Simon Pulse edition August 2006
10 9 8 7 6 5 4
Library of Congress Control Number 2005933856
ISBN-13: 978-1-4169-1810-3
ISBN-10: 1-4169-1810-8

THE NEW GIRL

prologue

*B*ye, Anna.

Good-bye.

Look at her down there, all crumpled. Her dress all crumpled.

She wouldn't like that. She was always so neat.

She wouldn't like the blood, so dark and messy.

You were always so perfect, Anna. You were always so bright and shiny, as if you were sparkly new every day.

"My Diamond," Mom always said.

And who was I, then?

Who was I while you were Little Miss Perfect?

Well, you're perfect now. You're perfectly dead, ha ha.

I shouldn't laugh. But it was so easy.

I never dreamed it would be so easy. Oh, I dreamed about it a lot. I dreamed it and wished it, and, oh, did I feel guilty.

But I never knew it would be easy.

One push.

One push, and down you go.

Look at you down there, all crumpled. So perfectly crumpled.

And now the front door is opening. They are returning. And I am starting to cry.

It is a horrible tragedy, after all.

A horrible tragic accident.

I must cry for you now. And I must run and tell them.

"Anna's dead, Mom! Come quickly! It's all too horrible—but Anna's dead!"

chapter

1

When Cory Brooks saw the new girl for the first time, he was standing on his head in the lunchroom.

Actually, he was standing on his head and one hand while balancing a full lunch tray in his free hand, his black Converse high-tops reaching straight up to where his head would normally be.

A few seconds earlier David Metcalf, Cory's best friend and fellow daredevil from the Shadyside High gymnastics team, had suggested that Cory couldn't perform this feat.

"That's too easy, man," Cory had said, shaking his head. Cory never passed up an opportunity to prove David wrong. He hesitated for only a second, running his hand back through his curly black hair and looking across the large, crowded room to make sure no teachers were watching. Then he flipped over in midair, landed, and balanced on his head and hand, without even tilting the loaded tray.

And now David was applauding and whistling his approval from a nearby table, along with several other laughing, cheering spectators. "Now do it no hands!" David called.

"Yeah, do it!" Arnie Tobin, another gymnastics team pal, urged.

"Do it with no head!" another joker yelled. Everyone laughed.

Cory, meanwhile, was beginning to feel a little uncomfortable. The blood was rushing to his head. He felt a little dizzy, and the top of his head began to ache from pressing against the hard tile floor.

"I dare you to eat your lunch like that!" David called, always challenging Cory on to greater glories.

"What's for dessert? Upside-down cake?" a girl yelled from near the windows. Several kids groaned and hissed their disapproval of this bad joke.

"Cory—lookin' good!" someone shouted.

"What is going on?" called an alarmed voice, the voice of a teacher.

The jokes, the loud voices, the cheers and laughter all seemed to fade when the new girl floated into Cory's view. She was so pale, so blond, so light, so beautiful, at first he thought he was imagining her. All the blood rushing to his head must be causing him to see things!

She was walking against the far wall, heading quickly to the double doorways. Cory caught only a glimpse of her, upside down. She stopped to stare at him. He saw pale blue eyes. His eyes connected with hers. Did she know he was staring back at her? Was she smiling or frowning? It was impossible to tell from his position. Then she shook her blond head, as if purposefully breaking the connection, and vanished from his view.

Those eyes.

Who is she? Cory thought. She's incredible!

Thinking about the new girl, he forgot to concentrate on the delicate balance that was keeping him upright. The tray fell first. Then Cory fell, his face sliding messily into his food, his chest hitting the floor hard, his long legs sprawling behind him.

The room erupted in laughter and sarcastic applause.

"Do it again!" Arnie Tobin's voice boomed. Arnie could outshout any crowd.

David hurried over to help Cory up. "Any more bright ideas?" Cory groaned, pulling spaghetti and tomato sauce out of his hair.

"Next time just get a sandwich," David said, laughing. He had carrot-colored hair, and freckles almost as orange, and he had a whooping, high-pitched laugh that could make dogs perk up their ears for miles around.

Cory used the front of his T-shirt to wipe spaghetti sauce from his face. When he looked up, Mrs. Mac-Reedy, the lunchroom monitor, was in front of him. She didn't say anything. She just shook her head.

"Sorry about that," Cory said, feeling more than a little foolish.

"About what?" Mrs. MacReedy asked, keeping a straight face.

Cory laughed. Thank goodness Mrs. MacReedy had a good sense of humor!

"It was all Arnie's idea," David told her, pointing back to the table where Arnie was busily shoving pretzel sticks into his mouth three at a time.

"I don't think Arnie's ever had an idea," Mrs. MacReedy said, still straight-faced. Then she gave Cory a quick wink and walked away.

Still dripping with noodles and tomato sauce, Cory bent down to pick up the tray. "Hey, David, who was that girl?"

"What girl?"

"The blond girl. The one who walked out while—"

"Who?" David seemed confused. He picked up Cory's scattered silverware and tossed it onto the tray. "A new girl?"

Cory groaned. "Didn't you see her?"

"No. I was watching you making a total dork of yourself."

"Me? It was your idea!"

"It wasn't my idea to do a face dive into a plate of spaghetti."

"She's blond and she was wearing a pale blue dress."

"Who?"

"The girl I saw."

"You saw a girl wearing a *dress* to school?"

"You don't believe me, huh?" Cory looked to the doorway as if she might still be there. But then his stomach growled, and he remembered he'd just ruined his lunch. "Hey, David, you got any money? I'm starving."

"Don't look at me, man," David said, grinning and backing away.

"Come on. You owe me." Cory put the tray down on an empty table and started to come after him.

"No way, man."

"Where's your lunch? We'll split it." Cory changed direction and headed toward David's table.

"*My* lunch? Forget it. I haven't—"

Cory took the apple off David's tray, then grabbed a handful of pretzel sticks from Arnie's.

"Hey—I need those!" Arnie protested, making a futile swipe to get them back.

"Be a pal," Cory said through a mouthful of apple. "We've got practice after school, right? If I don't eat, I'll be too weak to climb onto the balance beam."

"Break my heart," Arnie said as he broke off the pretzels in Cory's hand and shoved the halves quickly into his own mouth. "Maybe the rest of us will stand a chance."

Cory detected more than a little resentment from Arnie. He felt bad about that, but what could he do? He couldn't help it if he was a more talented gymnast than his teammates. He had been on the varsity gymnastics team since his freshman year at Shadyside. And Coach Welner really thought he had a chance of making the all-state championships the following spring.

It's a good thing Coach Welner didn't see me fall into my lunch, Cory thought. He finished off the last of Arnie's pretzel sticks and slurped up the last few drops of David's chocolate milk, then crushed the cardboard container in his hand.

"A well-balanced lunch," he said, hiccuping.

Arnie was busy showing David a new way to slap someone five. He had a serious look on his normally grinning face, and he was slapping David's hand again and again, trying to get it just right. "Not like that, jerk," he kept saying.

Cory couldn't figure out who was the jerk. "Later," he told them, tossing the crushed milk carton into a trash basket halfway across the room. They didn't look up.

He headed toward the double doors, ignoring some kids who were laughing about his stained shirt and the congealed tomato sauce in his hair. "Hey, Cory— think fast!" Someone threw a milk carton at him. It bounced off a table and hit the floor.

He didn't turn around. He was thinking about the girl in the blue dress again. He had seen her for only a few seconds, upside down. But he knew she was the most beautiful girl he had ever seen.

Hauntingly beautiful.

The phrase popped into his head.

He realized he was looking for her as he headed down the hall to his locker.

Where is she? Who is she? I didn't imagine her— did I?

"Hey, Cory—you swim in your lunch?"

He didn't turn around to see who that was. He realized he must look pretty bad. Suddenly he hoped he wouldn't run into the girl now. He didn't want her to see him with tomato sauce in his hair and all over his shirt.

He stood in front of his locker, trying to decide what to do. Was there time to head down to the showers? He looked at his watch. No. The bell for fifth period would ring in less than two minutes. Maybe he could cut English. No. Mr. Hestin was explaining the term paper assignment today.

Lisa Blume walked up and began turning the combination lock to open her locker. She pulled the lock open, then looked at him. "You look great."

"Thanks." He looked down at his shirt. "This remind you of when we were little kids?"

"No. You were neater then." She laughed.

Cory and Lisa had lived next door to each other in the North Hills section of town for their entire lives. They had played together since they were toddlers. Their two families were so close, they were like one big family.

Living so close together, Cory and Lisa had managed to stay friends even through those years when boys only play with boys and girls only play with girls. Now, as teenagers, they knew each other so well, they were so comfortable with each other, their friendship seemed a natural part of life.

Lisa had dark good looks, long black hair that tumbled in curls down to her shoulders, black, almond-shaped eyes, and dark lipsticked lips that curled into a half smile whenever she said something funny, which was often. A lot of kids said she looked like a movie star. Lisa pretended not to be flattered by the comparison, but she was secretly pleased.

Now she stared at Cory in front of their lockers. "I was standing on my head in the lunchroom," he told her as if that fully explained his appearance.

"Not again," she said. She bent down to pick up

some books from the floor of the locker. "Who were you showing off for this time?"

Her question annoyed him. "I didn't say I was showing off. I just said I was standing on my head."

"David dared you to. Right?"

"How'd you know?"

"Lucky guess." She stood up, her arms filled with texts and notebooks. "You can't go into class like that. You smell like a pizza."

"What can I do?"

"Here. You can borrow a T-shirt." She bent down again to rummage in the cluttered locker.

"A girl's shirt? I can't wear a girl's shirt!" He grabbed the sleeve of her sweater and started to pull her up.

She pulled out of his grasp. "It's not a girl's shirt. It's from the Gap. It's for girls or boys. You know. It's just a shirt." She pulled the black-and-white-striped T-shirt out and tossed it up to him. "But wash your hair before you put it on."

The warning bell rang. Locker doors slammed. The hall grew quiet as kids disappeared into their fifth-period classes.

"Get real. How can I wash my hair?"

She pointed to the water fountain across the hall. He smiled at her gratefully. "You're smart, Lisa. I always said you were smart."

"That's a real compliment coming from a guy who puts his head in his spaghetti," she said, her mouth sliding into that familiar, wry half smile.

"Hold the water on for me," he said, walking quickly to the low white fountain. He looked down the hall to make sure no one was watching. The hall was nearly deserted.

"No way, Cory. I don't want to be late." She followed him anyway. "And I certainly don't want to be seen with you."

"You're a pal, Lisa."

He didn't see her frown. She hated that word. She hated to be a pal. She sighed and turned the water knob. Then she stood there hoping that no one would come by as he plunged his head into the fountain and frantically struggled to scrub the dried sauce from his tangled curls.

The bell rang. She let go of the fountain. "Cory, I've got to go."

He stood up, water pouring down his face. "Good thing the water in this fountain never gets cold," he said. He pulled off the stained T-shirt and dried his hair with it.

"Cory—really. I don't want to be late." She tossed the clean T-shirt at him and, struggling to hold on to her armload of books, ran to class.

The striped shirt fell onto the floor in front of Cory's sneakers. Still rubbing his hair dry with the dirty shirt, he bent over to pick it up.

When he stood up, he saw her again.

First he saw her blue dress. Then he saw her blond hair.

She was halfway down the hall, hurrying to class.

There was something strange about the way she moved. Her feet didn't make a sound as she ran. She was so light she seemed to be floating a few inches above the ground.

"Hey, wait—" he called to her.

She heard him. She stopped and turned her head, her blond hair swirling behind her. Once again her blue eyes connected with his. What was that in her eyes? Was it fear?

Her lips moved. She was saying something to him, but he couldn't hear her.

"Please don't."

Is that what she had said?

No.

That wasn't it. That couldn't be it. Cory was a terrible lip reader.

"Please don't?"

No.

What had she really said? Why did she look so frightened?

"Please, wait—" he called.

But she vanished into a classroom.

chapter

2

Cory slammed the gym locker shut and angrily pounded his fist against it.

"Hey, what's the matter with you, man?" David asked, still in his practice sweats.

"I stink!" Cory shouted. "I looked like a spaz on the bars today."

"So what else is new?" David said with a shrug. "At least you didn't sprain your ankle." He rubbed the ankle, which was swollen nearly to the size of a softball.

"Later," Cory muttered disgustedly. He tossed his wet towel over David's head and angrily shoved his way out through the locker room door. He'd just had the worst practice of the year, maybe of his life. And he knew why.

It was the new girl.

Cory had been looking for her for three days. He hadn't seen her since that brief moment in the hall before fifth period on Monday. But he hadn't been able to get her out of his mind ever since. She was just so beautiful!

He had even dreamed about her that first night.

In the dream he was eating lunch in school. She seemed to float across the lunchroom. She came up to his table, her blue eyes shimmering like the ocean in sunlight. She leaned down and her hair fell over his face, soft and fragrant.

She started to kiss his face, his cheek, his forehead, his other cheek, soft kisses, so soft he couldn't feel them.

He wanted to feel her kisses. He tried to feel them. But he couldn't feel a thing.

He reached up to touch her face. His hand seemed to go right through her.

And he woke up.

The dream stayed with him. It should have been a nice dream, an exciting dream. But it wasn't. There was something eerily cold about the dream. Why couldn't he feel her kisses or touch her face?

For the next three days he had looked for her in the lunchroom and in the halls between classes. He had even waited by the front doors after school, hoping to get a glimpse of her. But she had never appeared. And none of the guys Cory had asked knew who she was or even remembered seeing her.

Now, as he trudged through the empty corridor, he tried to think about why his timing had been so off during gymnastics practice, but her face kept floating into his mind. And once again he imagined her floating across the hall.

"Are you real?" Cory asked aloud, his voice echoing off the tile walls.

"Yeah, I'm real. But what are you?" a girl's voice replied, nearly startling him out of his Converse.

"Huh?" He spun around to find Lisa behind him, a questioning look on her face.

"Talking to yourself these days?"

He could feel his face reddening. "What are *you* doing here? It's after five o'clock."

"It's my school, too, you know. I can stay as long as I like. You jocks think you own the place."

He shrugged. He wasn't in the mood to joke around with her.

"I was working on the *Spectator*. We were pasting it up today." Lisa was assistant editor of the Shadyside High School paper. "I suppose you were doing flip- flops in the gym?"

"It's not flip-flops," he said grumpily. "We have a match against Mattewan Friday night."

"Good luck," she said, punching his shoulder. They're pretty good, right?"

"They're not that good."

They walked down the hall, their footsteps echoing loudly. At their lockers they stopped to pull out jackets and backpacks.

"You going home?" Lisa asked. "Want company?"

"Sure," he said, although he really didn't.

They walked out the back doorway and stepped down into the teachers' parking lot. Beyond the parking lot stood the football stadium, a concrete oval with long wooden bleachers on two sides. And behind the stadium stood Shadyside Park, a wide, grassy park dotted with ancient oaks and sycamores and sassafras trees, sloping gradually down to the banks of the Cononnonka River, actually a narrow, meandering stream.

The nearness of the park made it an afternoon hangout for just about everyone who didn't have an after-school job. It was great for meeting friends, relaxing, enjoying after-school picnics or impromptu parties, studying, making out, playing endless games of Frisbee, taking an afternoon siesta, or just staring at squirrels or the slow-flowing river.

But not tonight. The wind was cold and gusty, and it swirled tangles of brown leaves in fast circles over the parking lot. Zipping their down jackets against the unexpected cold, Cory and Lisa looked up to a sky that was heavy and dark, a November sky, a snow sky.

"Let's go the front way," he said. They headed around toward the front of the school. She leaned against him as they walked. He figured she was trying to keep warm.

"Guess it's really winter," she said.

They turned up Park Drive and headed toward North Hills, a walk they had made together thousands of times. Tonight seemed different to him somehow. He guessed he was just in a bad mood.

They were silent for a long time, leaning up the hill, the gusting wind first behind them, then blowing hard in their faces. Then they both spoke at once.

He: "Have you seen a girl with blond hair and—"

She: "Are you doing anything this weekend? Saturday night?"

They both stopped talking at the same time, then started again at the same time.

She shoved him. "You go first."

He shoved her back, but not as hard. "No. You."

A car horn honked at them. Probably someone from school. A dark blue Honda Accord sped by. It was too dark to see who was inside.

"I asked if you were doing anything Saturday night," she said, leaning against him again.

"No. I don't think so."

"I'm not either," she told him. Her voice sounded funny, a little tense. He decided it was just because of the wind.

"Have you seen a girl with blond hair and big blue eyes?" he asked.

"What?"

"A very pretty girl, but strange-looking. Kinda old-fashioned. Very pale."

She let go of his arm. He didn't see the disappointed look on her face. "You mean Anna?" she asked.

He stopped walking and turned to face her, his expression suddenly excited. The streetlights flickered on. It looked as if he were lighting up because of her answer. "Anna? Is that her name? You know her?"

"She's a new girl. Very pale. Blond. Has her hair just brushed straight back with a barrette in front? Wears dresses all the time?"

"Yeah. That's her. Anna. What's her last name?"

"I don't know," Lisa snapped, then regretted revealing how annoyed she was. "Corwin, I think. Anna Corwin. She's in my third-period physics class."

"Wow," he said, still not moving, the trees casting

17

shadows across his face as they bent in the wind. "You know her. What's she like?"

"No, Cory, I don't know her. I told you. She's a new girl. I don't know her at all. She never says a word in class. Sits in the back row, as pale as a ghost. She's absent a lot. Why are *you* so hot to know her?"

"What else do you know?" Cory asked, ignoring her question. "Come on."

"That's it," Lisa said impatiently. She started walking on ahead of him, taking long strides.

He ran to catch up. "I thought I made her up," he said.

"No. She's real," Lisa replied. "She doesn't look real. But she's real. You in love with her or something? Oh. I know. David and you made a bet to see which one could get a date with her first." She shoved him again, nearly knocking him off the sidewalk. "I'm right, aren't I? You two always pick on the new girls."

Again he didn't seem to hear her. "Don't you know anything else about her? Whose homeroom is she in? Where does she live?"

"Oh. Yeah. I did hear that. She transferred here from Melrose. Her family moved into a house on Fear Street."

"Fear Street?" Cory stopped short, suddenly chilled.

Fear Street, a narrow street that wound past the town cemetery and through the thick woods on the south edge of town, had a special meaning for everyone in Shadyside. The street was cursed, people said.

The blackened shell of a burned-out mansion—Simon Fear's old mansion—stood high on the first block of Fear Street, overlooking the cemetery, casting eerie shadows that stretched to the dark, tangled woods. Terrifying howls, half-human, half-animal, hideous cries of pain, were said to float out from the mansion late at night.

People in Shadyside grew up hearing the stories about Fear Street—about people who wandered into the woods there and disappeared forever; about strange creatures that supposedly roamed the Fear Street woods; about mysterious fires that couldn't be put out, and bizarre accidents that couldn't be explained; about vengeful spirits that haunted the old houses and prowled through the trees; about unsolved murders and unexplained mysteries.

When Cory and Lisa were kids, their friends liked to dare one another to go for a walk on Fear Street at night. It was a challenge few kids were willing to accept. And those who did never stayed on Fear Street for long! Now, even though Cory was older, the words *Fear Street* still brought a chill.

"I think Anna belongs on Fear Street," Lisa said, giving Cory her half smile. "She could haunt one of those old houses as good as any ghost."

"I think she's the most beautiful girl I've ever seen," he said, as if he felt he had to defend her against all attacks.

"So do you have a bet with David or what?" she asked.

"No," he snapped, lost in thought.

They reached their houses, dark shingled ranch houses, almost identical, set back far from the street behind tall hedges of evergreens, on wide manicured lawns, as were most of the houses in North Hills, the nicest section of town.

"About Saturday night—" she tried again.

"Yeah. Right. See you tomorrow," he said, and began jogging up the long, paved drive to his house.

Anna. Anna Corwin. The name repeated in his mind. What a nice, old-fashioned name.

"That's right, Operator. The family's name is Corwin. It's a new number. On Fear Street."

"I'm looking for it, sir," the Information operator said. There was a long silence.

Why am I so nervous just calling Information? Cory asked himself.

He had thought about Anna all through dinner. Now, up in his room, he had decided to get her phone number. I know I'm going to be too nervous to call her, he thought. I just want to get the number. In case I want to call her someday.

There was a long silence. He sat leaning over the desk in his room, pencil poised over the yellow pad he kept near the phone.

"Yes, here's the number. It's a new listing." The operator read him the number, and he scribbled it down.

"And what's the address on Fear Street, Operator?"

"We're not supposed to give that out, sir."

"Come on. I promise I won't tell anybody." Cory laughed.

Surprisingly, the operator laughed too. "I guess it's

okay. It's my last night, anyway. It's Four Forty-four Fear Street."

"Thanks a lot, Operator. You're a nice person."

"You're nice too," she said, and quickly clicked off.

Cory stood over his desk and stared at Anna's phone number on the yellow pad. Should he call it?

If he called her, what would he say?

Call her, Cory. Go ahead. Don't be such a chicken. She's only a girl, after all. Sure, she's the most beautiful girl you've ever seen. But she's only a girl.

He picked up the receiver. His hand was cold and clammy even though it was quite hot in his room. He stared at the number on the yellow pad until it blurred before his eyes.

No. I can't call her. What would I say? I'd just stammer around and sound like a jerk. She already thinks I'm a jerk after seeing me standing on my head in the lunchroom.

He put down the phone receiver.

No. I can't. I just can't.

Sure. Why not?

He picked up the receiver.

This is stupid. I'm going to make an idiot of myself.

He punched her phone number.

Put the phone down, Cory. Don't be a jerk.

It rang once. Twice.

Maybe she won't even remember who I am.

It rang again. Again.

Nobody home, I guess. Whew!

He let it ring four more times. He was just about to

hang up when he heard a click at the other end, and a young man's voice answered, "Yeah?"

"Oh. Hello." For some reason he wasn't expecting anyone but Anna to answer. His mouth was suddenly so dry, he wondered if he could speak.

"Yeah?"

"Is Anna there?"

"What?"

Who was this guy? Why did he sound so annoyed? Maybe Cory had woken him up.

"I'm sorry. Is this the Corwin house?" Cory asked.

"Yeah, it is," the young man rasped in his ear.

"Could I speak to Anna please?"

There was a very long silence.

"Sorry. This is the Corwins. But there's no Anna here."

The phone clicked off.

chapter
3

*W*hen Cory arrived at school the next morning, Anna Corwin was the first person he saw.

It was raining hard, a freezing rain driven by gusty winds. He ran into the building through the side door, his letter jacket pulled up over his head. His wet sneakers slid across the floor, and he nearly collided with her.

"Oh." He grabbed the wall and stopped. He pulled down his jacket and stared at her. Her locker was the first one next to the door. She was pulling books off the top shelf and didn't seem to notice that he had nearly run into her.

She wore a white sweater over a gray skirt. Her hair was tied back behind her head with a white ribbon.

She's so pale, he thought. It's like I can almost see through her skin.

Suddenly the young man's raspy voice on the phone

came back to him. *This is the Corwins. But there's no Anna here.*

Well, here she was.

What was that guy trying to prove? Why had he lied to Cory?

Maybe it was a jealous boyfriend, Cory thought. Or maybe Cory had dialed the wrong number, and the guy was just pulling a mean joke

"Hi," he said, swinging his backpack down off his shoulder. A stream of water poured from it, onto his already soaked sneakers.

She turned, surprised that someone was talking to her. Her eyes, those amazing eyes, looked into his, then quickly looked down. "Hello," she said. Then she cleared her throat nervously.

"You're new," he said.

Brilliant line. Cory. Wow, that's a real winner. You say two words to her and she already knows what a dork you are!

"Yes." she said. She cleared her throat again. Her voice was little more than a whisper. But she seemed pleased that he was talking to her.

"Your name is Anna, right? I'm Cory Brooks."

That's a little better, Cory. Just calm down, man. You're doing okay.

He reached out to shake hands. He had to touch her, to know for sure that she was real. But his hand was dripping wet. They both stared at it. He quickly brought it back to his side.

"Nice to meet you," she said, turning back to search for something in her locker.

"You moved onto Fear Street, right?" It was almost

time for the bell to ring, but he didn't want to leave her. It had taken so long to find her.

She cleared her throat. "Yes."

"You must be pretty brave. Have you heard all the scary stories about Fear Street? About the ghosts and things—"

"Ghosts?" Her eyes grew wide and her face filled with such sudden fright, he was immediately sorry he had said that. She seemed to grow even more pale. "What kind of stories?"

"Just stories," he said quickly. "Not all of them are true, I don't think."

Nice going, Cory. Was that the only thing you could think of to say? How feeble can you get?

"Oh," she said softly. The fear didn't leave her eyes.

She's so pretty, he thought. Everything about her is so soft, so light.

His dream about her came back to him. It made him feel a little embarrassed.

"Hey, Cory—lookin' good!" some guy called to him.

He turned to see who it was. It was just Arnie, giving him the okay sign from down the hall.

"Later, Arnie!" he called. He watched Arnie go into the wood shop, then turned back to Anna.

"I—uh—I called your house last night. I—I just wanted to say hi. Uh . . . a guy answered and said you didn't live there. Did I have the wrong phone number, or—"

"No," she whispered, closing her locker and locking it.

Then she turned without looking back at him and ran down the hall, disappearing into the crowd of kids heading to homeroom.

"Good mat routine," Coach Welner said, giving Cory a hearty slap on the back. Cory, still breathing hard, grinned back at the coach. He knew he had done a good routine, but it was always nice to hear it from the coach. Mr. Welner, a stern, powerful-looking man with a body builder's physique even though he was in his late fifties, was sparing with his compliments. So when he said something nice, it meant something.

Behind them the match against Mattewan, the first match of the season, continued. Cory looked to the bench for David, wondering if his friend had witnessed his near-perfect routine. Then he remembered that David had sprained his ankle at the last practice. David was somewhere up in the bleachers feeling sorry for himself and being miserable.

"Now, don't press too hard on the rings," Coach Welner warned. "You've been pushing yourself, trying to go too fast up there, and it's been throwing you off your rhythm."

"Yeah," Cory said, still trying to catch his breath.

"You feel nervous?" the coach asked, staring at Cory as if trying to see the nervousness in his eyes.

"No. Not really. Just excited."

"Good. That's what we want." Mr. Welner seemed very pleased. "Just remember—don't push it. Easy does it." He turned away from Cory and let out a loud groan. "Get up, Tobin. You can rest later!"

Arnie had just done the backflip to finish his mat

routine and had landed flat on his backside. The twenty or thirty spectators in the bleachers were laughing their heads off. Arnie's face turned bright scarlet as he pulled himself up and slumped off the mat.

Coach Welner closed his eyes and shook his head disgustedly. Arnie's slip wasn't going to help the Shadyside team score. And the floor routine was the best part of Arnie's program. He was a complete klutz on the rings, and his parallel bar work was uneven to say the least.

The Mattewan guys were midgets compared to Cory and his teammates. But that gave them an advantage. They were light and strong and agile.

A guy like Arnie should be playing tackle on the football team, Cory thought. Whatever made him want to be a gymnast?

Whatever made Arnie decide to do anything? He was one of the flakiest guys Cory had ever known. He just grinned his way through life, seemingly without ever having a serious thought cross through his mind.

"Okay, Brooks." Coach Welner's voice broke into Cory's thoughts. "Go show 'em how it's done."

Cory took a deep breath and headed to the rings. For some reason they always looked so much higher at a real competition than in practice.

He shut the world out as he started his routine. He didn't need his brain. The moves were all locked in his muscles. After practicing these moves thousands and thousands of times, he was like a machine, a smoothly running machine.

Okay. Up. And over.

Very smooth, Cory. Now faster. Get ready. Here comes the hard part. Up, up . . .

And he saw Anna sitting in the bleachers.

Was it really Anna?

No. It couldn't be—could it?

. . . And over. And again. Stop. Reverse . . .

No. It was another blond girl.

The eyes. Those were her eyes.

Yes. It was Anna. What a surprise! She was staring up at him with those blue eyes.

She's watching me, he thought. She came to watch me.

He stared back at her. And he slipped. And dropped hard to the floor.

He didn't feel any pain. He was just confused. He didn't really fall, did he? He didn't really blow the whole routine just because a certain girl had caused him to lose his concentration?

"I'm falling for her!" he said aloud, laughing as he slowly climbed to his feet.

"What's so funny, Brooks?" Coach Welner was shouting.

"I'm falling for her," Cory repeated to himself. It was the second time he had fallen because of her, the second time he had embarrassed himself in front of a lot of people.

Was that true love, or what?

"What's so funny, Brooks?" Coach Welner looked concerned. "Are you hysterical or something? You didn't hit your head, did you?"

"I'm okay," Cory said, kicking the edge of a mat. "I just slipped, that's all."

"There'll be other matches," Coach Welner said. He suddenly looked very tired. "This one's a comedy act. Go shower, Brooks. Then go home and forget about today."

"Right, Coach." Cory looked up to the bleachers.

He remembered just where she was sitting—in the center of the third row.

But she wasn't there now. He stared at an empty space in the row.

His heart sank. Had she been there in the first place? He hadn't imagined her, had he? Was he cracking up because of this girl?

No. Of course not.

"I have to talk with her," he told himself. "I have to call her again."

chapter

4

Cory stared at the calendar hanging over his desk. Saturday night. Saturday night, and I'm sitting up here alone in my room, iPod blasting in my ears, staring at my desk, not even hearing the music, thinking about Anna Corwin.

A guy could get pretty depressed, he told himself. He tore off the iPod headphones and tossed them onto the desk.

Anna. Anna. Anna.

It's spelled the same both ways.

Brilliant, Cory. Just brilliant. Your mind really is turning to cheese, isn't it!

He knew he had to stop thinking about her. But how could he? She kept floating into his thoughts no matter what he did. He had liked other girls before—but never like this!

He leaned over and grabbed the phone. "I'll ask her to a movie or something," he told himself. "If I can just get to know her a little, maybe I won't be so crazy, so obsessed."

Those eyes. That whisper of a voice, as faint as the wind.

No. Stop. I can't call her on a Saturday night.

You can't call a girl on a Saturday night.

She's probably out.

I'll try her anyway, he decided. She seemed so pleased when I talked to her at her locker.

No, I can't call her. She'll be insulted. She'll think I'm calling on a Saturday night because I know she wouldn't be out with somebody.

I'll call David instead. Maybe he and I can go down to the mall and check out the action.

No. David can't go anywhere. He's hobbling around with crutches because of his ankle.

Call her, Cory. She'll be thrilled to hear from you.

Oh, sure. Thrilled. The klutz who always falls on his face when she looks at him.

He put down the receiver. Not tonight. No way.

I know. I'll catch her at her locker on Monday, maybe ask her to the basketball game next Friday.

He felt a lot better. He had a plan.

Now what should I do? The clock on his desk said eight-twenty. His parents had a hot Scrabble game going downstairs with Lisa's parents. Cory decided maybe he'd wander next door and see if Lisa was doing anything.

"Lisa home?" he called into the den, pulling on a sweatshirt.

"Yes, she is," Mrs. Blume called. "Why don't you

go over and keep her company? She was kinda down in the dumps because she didn't have a date tonight."

"Okay," Cory said, grabbing a bag of potato chips and a box of chocolate chip cookies off the kitchen shelf to take with him. There was never anything to eat at the Blumes' house. That was probably the real reason Lisa was depressed. She was probably starving, he figured.

I can talk to her about Anna, Cory told himself. He was eager to discuss Anna with someone. Whenever he brought up the subject with David or Arnie, they just teased him and made bad jokes.

"How'd the match with Mattewan go?" Mr. Blume called.

"Don't ask him that," Cory heard his mom say.

"Don't ask me that," Cory repeated.

"He fell on his keester," Cory's dad said in a whisper loud enough to be heard across the street. They all laughed.

"Thanks, Dad," Cory said. "Thanks a bunch."

Holding the cookies and potato chips in one arm, he pulled open the back door and stepped out into a frosty night. A sliver of a moon was partially hidden by thin wisps of clouds. That moon is so pale, he thought. It's the same color as Anna's hair.

Uh-oh, Cory. You'd better watch it, man. You're starting to see her everywhere—even in the moon! You're getting weird, man. Too weird. You've got to cool it.

He had to knock three times before Lisa opened the back door. She was wearing cut-off jeans and an enormous old white shirt that must have been her dad's. "Oh, hi," she said, sighing. "It's only you."

"Who'd you think?"

"I thought it was a burglar. You know, someone exciting." She backed up so that he could walk in. She smiled. "I'm only kidding. I'm glad you came over."

He held up the food packages.

"Now I'm really glad," she said, grabbing them both out of his hands. "I'm starving!"

He followed her into the den and sat down on the brown leather couch against the wall. She poured the potato chips into a big ceramic bowl and sat down next to him. "Another fabulous Saturday night."

"What were you doing?" he asked, grabbing a handful of chips and dropping them down into his mouth one by one from above. They tasted better that way, he thought.

"Nothing. I rented a movie, but I haven't started it yet. Want to watch it with me?"

"I don't know. What is it?"

She walked over to the counter under the TV and held up a DVD box. He gave her a double thumbs-down. "I'm not into *Lord of the Rings.*"

"Neither am I," she said, sighing again. "I got to the video store late. Everything was gone."

She slumped back down onto the couch, closer to him this time. They both reached out for more potato chips at the same time. Her hand grabbed his. She quickly let go. He didn't notice that she looked embarrassed.

"So how are things, Cory?" she asked, turning to face him. Their knees touched.

"Not great," he said, shrugging.

She put her hand on his arm. He could feel the warmth through his sweatshirt. "Poor baby. What's your problem?"

"Oh, I don't know. Nothing really. Everything."

She tsk-tsked. They didn't say anything for a while.

She moved her hand up to his hair and began to finger his curls. "I heard about the gymnastics match," she said softly.

"I blew it," he muttered, shaking his head. "I just blew it."

She leaned against him, still rolling her finger lightly in his hair. "Don't be so tough on yourself, Cory. It's only the first competition." She shoved the potato chip bowl aside and scooted even closer to him.

"Anna Corwin was there," he said. "I saw her watching me, and I was so surprised, I guess I lost my concentration."

"What?"

"I said Anna Corwin was there. I saw those blue eyes staring at me and—"

"Creep."

"What?"

"Nothing. I didn't say anything." She pulled away from him and jumped to her feet. He looked up, bewildered. Why did she look so angry?

"Have you ever talked with Anna?" he asked.

She stood over him and crossed her arms in front of her. "Cory, I think you should go home."

"Huh? I just got here."

"No. Really. Go home. Okay?"

"But why?"

"I—I'm just not in the mood for company. Okay? I'll see you in school Monday. I just don't feel like talking tonight."

He got up slowly, still confused. "Okay. Sorry you're not feeling well. Should I leave the chips and cookies?"

She glared at him. She picked up the box of cookies. For a second he thought she was going to fling it at him. But she put it in his hand. "Take the cookies. I'll finish the chips. What the heck? Might as well get fat. Why not?"

"Glad I could cheer you up," he said, trying to get her to smile. She didn't.

A few seconds later he was back outside, heading over the frosty hard grass to his house. A few seconds after that he was back in his room, sitting on his bed, trying to figure out what to do for the rest of the night.

What was Lisa's problem? he wondered. It wasn't like her to be so moody. She wasn't depressed just because she didn't have a date. Something else had to be bothering her. But what?

He glanced at his desk clock: nine twenty-five. His eye fell on the yellow pad beside the phone. He walked over to the desk and stared down at Anna's phone number.

Without stopping to think about it, without giving himself time to get nervous, time to talk himself out of it, he punched her number.

It rang once, twice, the sound seeming very far away even though it was just on the other side of town.

After the third ring he heard a click. Someone picked it up. A soft female voice said, "Corwins. Hello?"

"Hello, Anna?"

There was a long pause. Cory listened to the static on the line.

"Who?" the woman's voice repeated.

"May I speak to Anna please?"

"Ohhh!" The woman let out a loud gasp.

More silence. Then Cory heard a loud screech in the background. What was that awful sound? It sounded like a girl screaming.

Yes. Must be the TV, he told himself.

It had to be the TV.

"Why do you call here asking for Anna?" the woman demanded angrily.

"Well, I just—"

Again Cory heard the girl shrieking in the background. *"Let me talk! It's for me! I know it's for me!"*

The woman ignored the girl's cries. "Why do you call to torture me like this?" she asked Cory, her voice trembling.

"Well, is Anna there?" Cory asked.

"No, no, no!" the woman insisted. "You *know* Anna isn't here! You *know* she isn't! Stop. Please—stop!"

He heard the beginning of another scream. Then the phone clicked off.

chapter

5

Cory listened to the hum of the dial tone for a while as he waited for his heart to stop pounding. He played the conversation with the woman over and over again in his mind until the words became a blur. And over the blur he heard the screams, the girl's screams of protest in the background.

Let me talk. It's for me! I know it's for me!

What was going on there?

Cory's mind whirred with crazy, frightening thoughts. What were they doing to Anna? Why wouldn't they let her come to the phone? Why did they keep insisting she wasn't there?

Fear Street. Was it claiming another victim?

Was Anna being held prisoner in her own house? Were they torturing her?

"You've seen too many bad movies," he told himself. "You're being ridiculous."

Then what was the explanation?

"I'll go over there," he said aloud. The idea just popped into his mind. It seemed simple enough. He glanced at the desk clock. It was just a little after ten, still early.

He examined himself in the mirror on his closet door, straightened the sleeves on his sweatshirt, pushed his dark curly hair back from his forehead with his hands, and headed out of his room and down the stairs toward the den.

He stopped halfway down the stairs.

Hold on a minute. Do I really want to go to Fear Street—by myself? What if something horrible really is happening in that house? What if those screams were real?

The big local news story of a few weeks before suddenly flashed into his mind. A family of three had been found murdered in the Fear Street woods. No one was reported missing. No one came forward to identify them.

Just another Fear Street unsolved murder. . . .

Cory decided to call David and ask him to come along. David was sure to be sitting home, staring at his ankle, bored out of his mind. He needed a little excitement.

To Cory's surprise David thought the idea was a little strange. "Let me get this straight, Brooks," he said after Cory had explained their mission. "You want to drive over to Fear Street and break in on someone's horror movie to find a girl who isn't there in the first place."

"Right," Cory said.

"Okay. Sounds good to me," David replied. "Pick me up in ten minutes."

"Make it five," Cory said, and hung up before David could change his mind.

Good old David, Cory thought. I can always count on him to be as stupid as I am!

The Scrabble game was still going strong downstairs in the den. The board was nearly filled, and all four adults sat staring at it in silence, concentrating on finding a usable open space.

"I'm going out for a short while," he told his dad. "Which car can I take?"

"Kind of late, isn't it?" his mother asked without looking up from the board. She had a letter square in her hand, a blank, which she was rolling over and over between her fingers.

"It's only ten."

"Take the Taurus," his father said. "Don't take your mother's car."

"Where are you going?" his mother insisted.

"Just over to David's." It was partly true.

"Are you going to make a word, or what?" Mrs. Blume asked Cory's mom with that impatient tone everyone gets near the end of an endless Scrabble game.

"How's David doing?" Mr. Brooks asked.

"Bad," Cory told him. "He's on crutches. He's pretty depressed."

"Poor guy," Mrs. Blume muttered, staring at her letters.

"I pass," Mrs. Brooks said, sighing unhappily.

Cory grabbed the keys off the front counter and

headed out to the car. David lived about six blocks away in the northern corner of North Hills, almost to the river. It was a two-minute drive.

Cory knocked on the front door and waited. It took a long time for David to get to the door. "Sorry, man. I can't go with you" was his greeting.

"What do you mean?"

"I mean I can't go. My mom won't let me." He looked embarrassed.

"Hi, Cory," David's mother called from behind David in the hallway. "I really don't want David to go out tonight. He's got to stay off the ankle. Besides, he's getting a cold. You understand."

"Sure, Mrs. Metcalf," Cory said, unable to hide his disappointment. "A cold." He grinned at David. "We wouldn't want Mama's angel to catch a nasty cold, would we?"

David rolled his eyes and shrugged. "Give me a break."

"I'll call you later and let you know what happened on Fear Street," Cory said. "If you don't hear from me, send out the marines or the National Guard."

"Have you seen *Poltergeist?*" David asked. "If you go in that house, you might be sucked right into the TV screen!"

Cory didn't laugh. "You think this is all a big joke, don't you!"

David gave him an exaggerated, wide grin. "I think it's a riot."

"Well . . ." Cory turned and stomped down the flagstone walk back toward his car. "You're probably right."

Cory drove south on Park Drive and headed toward Fear Street. It was a cold and raw night. Thick clouds of fog drifted rapidly down from the hills. He turned up the heater and pushed on the radio. He needed some loud music to keep up his spirits.

"It's a Q-ROCK Beatles Blast!" the disc jockey screamed enthusiastically. "Twenty-four hours of Beatles hits in alphabetical order!"

Cory laughed. Why would anyone want to listen to music in alphabetical order?

He wished David were there to share the laugh. He wished David were there period. He really didn't like the idea of roaming around Fear Street on a cold, foggy night on his own. "Oh, well, I won't get out of the car," he told himself. "I'll just drive past the house and see what's going on."

The fog grew thicker as he passed Canyon Road and entered the valley. It was always misty at night down in this part of town, even in the summer. The car headlights seemed to hit the swirling mist and bounce back onto the windshield. He tried the brights, but they were worse.

An oncoming car swerved to miss him. Other drivers couldn't see either, Cory realized, a thought that didn't make him feel any more confident. "This is a mistake," he told himself.

But the fog lightened as he turned down Mill Road. A small Toyota, jammed with a least six teenagers, honked as it sped past him. They were probably coming from the deserted mill at the end of the road, a favorite makeout spot for Shadyside kids.

The dream about Anna in which she was kissing his

face flashed into his mind. He turned the radio up. Q-ROCK was up to the L's. They were playing "Love Me Do."

Tapping his hands against the wheel to the music, recreating the sexy dream in his mind, he nearly missed the turn onto Fear Street. He realized where he was and hit the brake hard, making a skidding turn across the wet pavement.

It seemed to grow darker as soon as he turned onto the narrow, curving street. Tall maples and oaks lined both sides, their bare creaking branches nearly forming an archway over the road, tangled limbs blocking much of the pale gray light from the streetlamps.

He couldn't see it in the dark, but he knew that he was passing Simon Fear's burned-out mansion. He sped up and turned up the heater. The houses, rambling old Victorians for the most part, were set far back from the road behind unkempt hedges or overlooking lawns still thick with swirling brown leaves.

"How am I ever going to find which house is hers?" Cory asked himself, wiping the inside of the windshield clear with his sweatshirt sleeve. He squinted out through the smeared glass, trying unsuccessfully to see a street number.

"What was her number?" he asked himself, beginning to panic. Had he driven all this way without even knowing her house number? No. It was 444. He remembered.

He pulled the car over to the side of the road and shifted into park. He turned off the headlights and waited for his eyes to adjust to the darkness. He could actually see a little better with the lights off.

He turned off the engine, opened the door, and slid out of the car. If he was going to find her house, he'd have to do it on foot. The numbers were on the front doors of the houses. There was no way he could read them from the car.

He shivered. The sweatshirt didn't offer much protection from the damp cold. He took a deep breath. The air smelled sour; decaying leaves most likely.

An animal howled nearby, a long, mournful wail.

"It doesn't sound like a dog," he told himself, looking in the direction of the sound but seeing nothing. "Could it be a wolf?"

The animal howled again. It sounded a little closer.

Cory suddenly remembered being on Fear Street before. He was a kid, nine or ten. His friend Ben had dared him to walk in the woods. Somehow he had gotten the courage to try. But he had walked for only a few minutes when something grabbed his shoulder.

Maybe it had been a tree branch. Maybe not. He had run screaming down the street. He had never been so scared in his life.

"Stop thinking about it," he said aloud.

His sneakers crunched over the gravel that lined the side of the road. He came to a metal mailbox tilting at an angle toward the street. Squinting in the darkness, he tried to read the faded name on its side. But it was too dark, and the letters were all peeled away.

The animal howled again. This time it sounded farther away. The wind suddenly stopped. The only sound now was the crunching of his sneakers. He passed a large weather-beaten house, its window shutters peeling and hanging at crazy angles. For some reason a rusting ship's anchor rested in the very center of the patchy lawn. An old station wagon, its rear bumper missing, two of its windows covered with cardboard, stood in the drive.

"Nice night for a stroll," Cory told himself. He started humming "Love Me Do" to himself. Then he started singing it. Why not? There was no one around to hear him. Fear Street was deserted. Nothing moved except the scrabbling brown leaves driven by the shifting wind.

One house was brightly lit. A porch light cast bright golden beams over the lawn, and all of the downstairs and second floor rooms seemed to be lighted. Was that Anna's house?

No. The sign on the porch said 442.

The wind picked up again, sending a chill down Cory's back. He shoved his hands into his jeans pockets to try to warm them. He had a sudden hunch and turned back to see if the car was okay. He couldn't see it. The street had curved too far.

Should he go back?

No. He'd come this far. The next house had to be Anna's.

If she lived there.

He began walking faster. The pavement beneath his sneakers was wet and slippery, and he slipped a couple of times but quickly regained his balance.

A ragged, low hedge bordered the yard of the next house. Was this the Corwin house? Cory couldn't find a mailbox. Oh. There it was. Down on the street. It had fallen off its pole.

He picked up the mailbox. There was a number on its side: 444. This was it. He dropped it back to the street and wiped his wet hands on his jeans.

The house was completely dark and silent. No sign of life. No car in the driveway. Cory peered over the low hedge to the front porch. A screen door hung open, banging against the side of the house when the wind blew. An overturned lawn chair was beside it.

Cory stepped to the edge of the drive. What now? Go up to the house and knock on the door? There doesn't seem to be anyone home.

He looked at the overgrown shrubs, the thick covering of unraked leaves, and tangles of waist-high grass and weeds. It didn't look as if anyone had lived there for years!

It's got to be the wrong house, he thought.

Then he heard something. Something moving across the gravel. A footstep.

He listened. The wind picked up. He couldn't hear anything. It must have been leaves. Or an animal of some sort.

He decided to walk back to the car. There was no point standing out in the cold staring at a deserted old house.

He heard another footstep, then another.

Someone was behind him.

Someone was following him, coming up fast.

Cory picked up his pace, started to jog, hoping to

leave the sounds behind, hoping it was just leaves, just a dog, just a lonely field cat.

But the footsteps came faster. Someone was chasing him. Someone was right behind him.

He started to turn around when a hand grabbed his shoulder.

chapter

6

Cory cried out and spun out of the man's grasp.

The man looked more startled than Cory. "Sorry. Didn't mean to scare you."

Cory stared at him, gasping for breath, his muscles tensed for a fight. Or for a fast escape.

He was a tall, powerful-looking man, wearing a faded gray slicker and a battered old tennis hat. He had a day's stubble of gray beard, and he smelled of stale cigarette smoke. "No need to be frightened," he said. He had a high-pitched voice for someone so big.

"Why—why'd you—" Cory was still too out of breath to talk. He backed up another few steps, relaxing a little but still eyeing the man warily.

"I saw you stop your car," the man said, pointing back in the direction of Cory's car. "I live down the street. I was walking Voltaire. That's my dog. I thought maybe you were lost or in trouble. So I came after you."

"Where's your dog?" Cory asked suspiciously.

The man frowned, seemingly annoyed by Cory's mistrust. "Voltaire doesn't like strangers," he said slowly. "He's very protective of his turf. I put him back in the house before I came to see if you needed help."

Cory was beginning to breathe normally again. But he knew he couldn't relax his guard. There was something strange about this neighbor, not just his appearance, but in his menacing stare, the way he kept looking Cory up and down, his face tight, expressionless.

"Car break down?" the man asked.

"No," Cory said.

"Then what are you doing out here? You lost?"

"Not exactly. I was looking for the Corwins."

"You found them," the man said, gesturing with his head toward the dark house. "You know them?"

"Well . . . not really."

"They're strange people. I wouldn't go up there uninvited, I don't think." The man scratched at his stubble.

"What do you mean?" Cory shivered. He'd never felt so chilled in his life.

"Just that."

"Oh."

They stood staring at each other for a long moment.

"They keep to themselves mostly," the man said. He put his hands in his slicker pockets and turned back toward the street. "If you're not lost or anything, guess I'll head back."

"Yes. I mean, no. I'm fine. Thanks," Cory said uncertainly. He looked up to the Corwin house. A light flickered on in an upstairs window.

So. Someone was home after all.

"They're pretty strange folks," the man repeated, walking quickly now. He turned around. "Of course, everyone's pretty strange on Fear Street." He chuckled as if he had just made a really good joke, and slipped off into the darkness.

Cory waited to make sure the man was really gone. Then he turned and headed slowly toward the car. He stopped and looked back to the house. The light was still on in the second-floor room.

Should he go up and knock on the door?

He'd come this far. Why not be brave? Why not just do it? Act now—think later. Why did he always have to go back and forth, think things out so carefully before he acted?

Besides, he'd have something good to tell David about later.

He imagined how his friend would make fun of him if he told him he just stood at the end of the drive and stared at the house. He'd probably hear about it for weeks. The jokes would never stop.

Okay, Cory. Go for it.

He began jogging up the Corwins' driveway. He jogged partly to get warm, partly because he knew he'd never go through with it if he didn't do it quickly.

A gymnast learns he has to be aggressive, he told himself. He has to grab on to the rings and push

49

himself where his body normally wouldn't go. As a gymnast, Cory was quick and sure.

But this wasn't gymnastics. This was life.

He jumped up onto the front porch, dodged past the overturned chair, slid on some long carpenter nails that were scattered over the porch floor, and nearly crashed right into the front door.

He steadied himself, leaning against the shingled front of the house, located the doorbell and, without hesitating, without giving himself a chance to back down, pushed it hard.

He didn't hear it ring inside the house. He pushed it again.

He straightened his sweatshirt and pushed back his hair with one hand.

The bell didn't make a sound. It must be broken.

He knocked, lightly at first, then harder.

Silence.

He cleared his throat, practiced a smile.

He knocked again.

This time he heard footsteps, someone hurrying down a stairway.

The door opened a crack. No light poured out. The house was dark inside. An eye stared out at Cory. The door opened a little wider. Two eyes stared suspiciously out.

The porch light flickered on, casting a pale yellow glow on the porch and front lawn.

A young man stood in the doorway. He had a very round face with puffy, round cheeks. His blue eyes were small and watery and set close to his bulby, round nose. Despite the fact that he appeared to be quite young, in his early twenties most likely, his blond hair was thinning, revealing a lot of forehead. It was tossed messily over his head. A rhinestone earring sparkled in one ear.

He stared at Cory for a long time without saying anything. Cory stared back uncomfortably. Finally he said, "Hi. I'm Cory Brooks. Is Anna home?"

The young man's watery eyes grew wide. His mouth twitched once in surprise. "Anna? What do you know about Anna?" His voice was raspy, as if he had a bad sore throat.

"I—uh—I go to Shadyside too."

"Shadyside? What's Shadyside?" the young man said, and then coughed for a long time, holding tightly on to the front door, a wheezing smoker's cough.

"It's the high school," Cory said when the young man finally stopped coughing. "I met Anna in school this week and—"

"That's impossible," the man interrupted, hitting the door frame with his fist. He glared at Cory. His eyes seemed to glow red in the porch light.

"No, really. I—"

"You didn't meet Anna in school. Anna isn't in school."

"Yes, she is," Cory insisted. "She—"

"You the one who called?"

"Well, yes. I—"

"Anna is dead," the young man rasped. "Don't come here again. Anna is DEAD!"

chapter

7

*H*e didn't remember driving home.

He remembered staring into the young man's watery eyes. He remembered the long, awkward silence, the pain on the young man's face.

He remembered the words. They repeated in his head over and over, like a record stuck in the same groove. *Anna is dead. Anna is dead. . . .*

He remembered uttering some kind of apology. "Sorry." That was it. That was all he could say. "Sorry." How stupid. How meaningless.

But what else could he say?

Then he remembered the scowl on the young man's puffy face, the shadows closing over him as the front door slammed shut. And Cory remembered running to his car, running to safety with the words following him. *Anna is dead. Anna is dead.*

He couldn't run fast enough to leave the words behind.

He remembered the chill wet air on his face, the crunch of dry brown leaves beneath his sneakers, the sharp twig that cut his ankle as he ran.

Stay away from Fear Street, he told himself.

What were you doing on Fear Street so late at night?

The stories are all true, and now you are one of them.

He remembered how his hand trembled as he tried to get the key into the ignition. And he remembered his panic when the car wouldn't start.

Then the motor had kicked over and he had sped away, his hands gripping the wheel as if it were a lifesaver in a storm-tossed ocean.

But he didn't remember the drive home. It was a blur of swirling yellow headlights and black roads. And he didn't remember sneaking back into the house, or silently tiptoeing up the stairs to his room, or getting undressed and climbing into bed.

He just remembered the young man's narrow, watery eyes. The pain in those eyes, pain mixed with hatred. And the words.

Anna is dead. Anna is DEAD!

He didn't fall asleep until after four in the morning. And then it was a light sleep, a fitful sleep filled with floating faces he didn't recognize and tilting car headlights that sometimes seemed to be heading right at him and sometimes seemed to shine right through him.

On Monday morning he skipped breakfast and hurried to school to look for Anna. He got there early, twenty minutes before the first bell would ring. He waited by her locker. There were a few other kids down the hall. They seemed to be yawning at each other, leaning against their lockers as if they would fall over if they didn't.

He tried opening Anna's locker, but the combination lock wouldn't budge. He sat cross-legged on the floor and waited. After a while the corridor became noisy and crowded as kids arrived. Some of them said hi to Cory as they walked past.

"What are you doin' down there, Brooks?" Arnie asked as he lumbered through the door.

"Just sitting," Cory told him.

The answer seemed to be enough for Arnie. He swung his bookbag at Cory, trying to knock him over. Cory dodged away. Arnie laughed and stomped down the hall.

Where is Anna?

Anna is dead.

Anna is a ghost.

But there are no such things as ghosts.

Her locker was real. He spun the dial and pulled at the lock again. The bell rang.

He climbed to his feet. He felt as if he weighed four hundred pounds. He hadn't been able to sleep for two nights in a row. The hallway was emptying quickly. Kids were hurrying to their homerooms. He had to hurry too. He had already been late twice this term, and he didn't want to get a detention.

But where was Anna?

She wasn't coming today.

Of course she wasn't coming today. Anna was dead.

But he had seen her with his own eyes. He had talked to her.

He made it to homeroom just as the bell rang. The rest of the morning was a struggle to keep his eyes open. Luckily, none of his teachers called on him in any of his classes. In fact, no one seemed to notice he was there.

Maybe I'm becoming a ghost, too, he told himself.

He looked for Anna in the hallway between classes, but he didn't see her. Just before lunch he ran into Lisa as they were depositing their bookbags in their lockers.

"Was Anna Corwin in physics this morning?" he asked her eagerly.

"Good morning to you too," Lisa said sarcastically.

"Oh. Sorry. Good morning, Lisa. Was Anna Corwin in physics this morning?"

She angrily slammed her locker shut. "No."

"Oh." Cory tossed his bookbag into his locker. He didn't see the annoyed look on Lisa's face. "Then I guess she was absent."

"You're a real Sherlock Holmes," Lisa said, shaking her head. She jammed the lock shut and started to walk away. But then she changed her mind and came back to the locker. "What's your problem, anyway?"

"Problem?" How did Lisa know he had a problem?

"Why are you acting so weird?"

"I'm not acting weird. I just—" He started to make some excuse, but then he decided to tell her. He had to tell someone. And she was his oldest friend, after all.

As they walked down to the lunchroom, he told her about the rest of his Saturday night.

He told her how he drove to Fear Street, how he knocked on the door, how the strange-looking young man told him Anna was dead.

Lisa listened to the story in silence, her face drawn in a tight frown of disapproval. But when Cory finished talking, the anger disappeared, replaced by concern. "Something's wrong here," she said softly, following him into the lunch line.

"A *lot* is wrong here!" Cory exclaimed. "I just can't stop thinking about—"

"I think you got the wrong house," she interrupted. She smiled, pleased with her idea.

"What are you talking about?"

"That's it. You got the wrong house. You woke this guy up. So he decided to play a mean joke on you." Lisa watched for Cory's face to brighten, waited for him to realize that her theory was a good one.

But his only reaction was a weary sigh. "Get real," he muttered gloomily. "I didn't have the wrong house."

"You don't know for sure," she insisted, although she could see this theory wasn't going to go over. "What did you think you were doing, anyway?" she asked, poking him in the ribs the way she'd been doing it since they were kids. "Why are you driving to this girl's house in the middle of the night? Why are you looking for her all day? Why are you so obsessed with Anna Corwin? There are other girls in the world, you know."

He didn't say anything. He seemed to be staring right past her.

"Cory—did you hear a word I said?"

"Yeah, sure," he answered quickly, still not looking at her. "You said the guy in the doorway was playing a mean joke on me."

Anna is dead. Some joke!

"Bye, Cory." She gave him an exaggerated handshake and started to leave.

"What about lunch?" he called after her.

"I'm not hungry anymore. Hey—you want to walk home after school?"

"Can't," he called to her. "Monday's the day I work in the office." A lot of kids did clerical work after school in the office. The pay wasn't too bad, and the work was easy, mostly copying and filing.

He watched her make her way through the crowded lunchroom to the double doorways that led to the hall Why had she accused him of acting weird? She'd been acting pretty weird herself, he decided. So temperamental. Always so angry at him. Why? What had he done to her?

Suddenly an idea formed in his head.

The office.

Of course. Why hadn't he thought of it before?

The office.

After school in the office he would be able to answer all his questions.

He got out of the lunch line and started toward the door. He decided to go outside and get some air, maybe walk a bit. He wasn't feeling hungry either.

Cory finished copying the announcement about

the faculty blood drive. He had one other photocopy to run off before his office chores were finished.

Moving more quietly and sneakily than he really needed to, he made his way to the door of the inner office and peered in. The room was empty. He had overheard that Mr. Sewall, the principal, had left early with a toothache. And one of the secretaries was out sick. That left only Miss Markins, who was busily typing away in the outer reception area.

The coast was clear. And would probably stay clear.

He slipped into the inner office and pulled the door nearly shut. His hand went for the light switch, but then he realized it might be a bad idea. Miss Markins was sure to notice it.

He crept over to the principal's desk in the center of the small office. Framed photographs of Mr. Sewall's two sons seemed to stare at him disapprovingly. Cory walked silently around the desk to get to the object of his search.

Against the back wall were the gray filing cabinets. They contained the permanent records of every student at Shadyside.

These were the sacred permanent records, the secret files that could make you a success in the world— or destroy your life forever.

At least, that's what most Shadyside High students were led to believe.

"I'm sorry—but this will have to go on your permanent record." If a teacher or Mr. Sewall ever said that to you, you knew you were doomed forever. Whatever it was, whatever crime you had committed, whatever error you had made would follow you for the rest of your life. There it would be, in your *permanent* record.

Cory ran his hand over the first row of file drawers, quickly scanning the little identification cards on the front. Just being in the same room with the permanent records made him nervous. The fact that he had no business in there and that he'd have to do some fast explaining if he was caught made him so nervous, he could barely read the ID cards.

He stopped his search for a second, held his breath, and listened. Miss Markins was still typing away. Whew. He allowed himself to breathe once again.

"I can't believe I'm doing this. What am I doing in here?" he asked himself, stooping low and pulling out a long file drawer on the bottom row.

He knew the answer to that question. He was going to take a look at Anna Corwin's permanent record. He was going to find out the truth about her. He was going to find out everything he could about her.

His fingers sifted quickly through the files. He knew this wasn't right. He knew it was crazy behavior. He knew he never did things like this. At least, before Anna he never did things like this.

Footsteps.

He took a deep breath.

He listened for her typing, but it had stopped.

He dived under Mr. Sewall's desk just as she entered the room.

"Safe!" he told himself. Or was he? Had she heard him in there?

He almost cried out. He had left the file drawer

open. If she saw it, she'd know he'd been in there.

She stood behind the desk. Her legs were three inches from his face. For a second he imagined reaching out and grabbing her knees just to see how loud she'd scream. Just for a laugh.

A last laugh before they took him away. Suspended him forever. Put it all on his permanent record.

He held his breath. It seemed as if he'd been holding it ever since he sneaked into this office. She was leaning over the desk, writing something. Leaving a note for Mr. Sewall, most likely.

I can't believe I'm sitting here under Mr. Sewall's desk, he told himself silently. But Anna's face flashed into his mind again. And he heard the words of the strange young man at the doorway of her house. And he remembered why he was there.

Miss Markins finished her note and walked out of the office without noticing the open file drawer. As soon as he heard her resume her typing, Cory darted out from under the desk and returned to the file drawer, moving his hands quickly through the C's.

What would Anna's file tell him? What truths would it reveal about this beautiful girl who had so completely taken over his thoughts?

Corn . . . Cornerman . . . His hands moved quickly, pushing the files back. At last! *Cornwall . . . Corwood . . . Corwyth . . .*

Wait a minute.

He went back through the last five or six. Then he moved forward nine or ten more.

He hadn't missed any. And none of them were filed

out of order. The files went from *Cornwall* to *Corwood*.

There was no file for anyone named Anna Corwin!

chapter

8

*"T*imberrr! Look at that guy go down!" Arnie's voice boomed over the cheers of the crowd.

"He's too tall!" David cried. "He's seven feet tall, and he's just a freshman!"

"He's still growing!" Arnie added.

They looked over at Cory, who was staring straight across the gymnasium.

"Hey, Brooks—Earth calling Brooks!" David shouted right in his ear. But Cory didn't respond.

The Shadyside cheerleaders did a quick routine during the time-out. Then the basketball game resumed. It wasn't much of a game. Westerville, with its seven-foot freshman center, was running the Shadyside Cougars off the floor.

"They have only one play—toss it to the big guy," David observed.

"I'd like to toss it to that cheerleader on the end!"

Arnie shouted, loud enough for half the auditorium to hear. "Oh, man. What a fox!"

David and Arnie both waited for Cory to add his opinion. But he didn't say anything. He looked at them as if seeing them for the first time. "Good game, huh?" he said, forcing a smile.

"What game are you watching?" Arnie snapped. "We're losing by twenty points."

"And the game isn't as close as the score!" David added. He and Arnie burst into riotous laughter, slapping each other high fives.

The weak, forced smile faded from Cory's face. He turned and started surveying the auditorium again.

"You're a lot of laughs these days, Brooks," Arnie said, reaching across David to punch Cory as hard as he could on the shoulder. "Aw, I'm goin' down to get a Coke." He pushed his way down the aisle and disappeared around the side of the bleachers.

"You feeling okay?" David asked. He had to ask it twice before Cory heard him.

"Yeah. Fine."

"Well, how come you missed practice this afternoon?"

"I don't know. Just forgot, I guess."

"Welner was furious. That's the second practice you missed this week, Cory. And the Friday practice is the most important—especially since we have a meet tomorrow."

"I know," Cory said, sounding annoyed. "Give me some slack, David. You're not my mother."

"Hey—" David looked really hurt. "I'm your teammate, aren't I? I'm your friend, aren't I?"

"So?"

"So—you tell me. What's your problem, Brooks?"

"Oh, nothing. Just—"

The crowd roared. All around them people jumped to their feet. Something had obviously gone Shady-side's way. But David and Cory had missed it. The cheerleaders came back on the floor. The bleachers were shaking under the deafening noise. Cory looked to the scoreboard. The Cougars were only behind by fifteen now. That must explain the excitement.

"It's that blond girl, isn't it?" David said when it became quiet enough to talk.

"I guess." Cory shrugged. He didn't really want to get into any big discussion with David. He felt bad. He really had forgotten about gymnastics practice. How was that possible? Was he really losing his mind over this girl?

"You going out with her?" David asked.

"I haven't seen her," Cory said, looking across the basketball floor.

"What?"

"You heard me. I haven't seen her all week. I looked for her every day, but she hasn't been in school."

"And that's why you're acting like a zombie?"

"Get off my case, Metcalf," Cory scowled.

"You're screwing up your gymnastics rating be-cause of a girl you don't know that you haven't seen? Well, that makes sense to me."

Cory didn't say anything. Then he suddenly blurted out, "I don't even know if she exists!"

He regretted saying it immediately. It didn't make

any sense, and he knew it. And now he had given David even more of an opportunity to put him down and give him a hard time.

But to Cory's surprise, David reacted with real concern. "What do you mean, Brooks? You told me you saw her—more than once. You told me you talked to her. You told me she's in Lisa's physics class. You told me all this stuff about her because that's all you talk about these days. So what do you mean, she doesn't exist?"

"I work after school in the office on Mondays. You know. So Monday afternoon I went into the permanent files and looked her up. There was no file for her!"

David looked shocked, but not for the reason Cory imagined. "You—you can get into the files?" he cried. "Great! What does mine say about me?"

"I didn't—"

"I'll give you ten bucks to look at my file. Better than that, I'll pay you back the ten bucks I owe you!"

"No deal," Cory said disgustedly. "You don't understand. I went to her house last week, and this guy said—"

The crowd groaned. Loud boos echoed off the tile walls. Cory's eye caught the scoreboard. Shadyside was losing by twenty-two.

Arnie pushed his way back into the row and plopped down beside David. "That guy's too tall," he said. He had spilled Coke down the front of his sweatshirt. "They've gotta raise the baskets!"

"Or lower the floor!" David said, and they both began to howl.

65

Cory stood up. "Guess I'm going," he told them. "This is a drag."

"You're a drag," Arnie said, grinning.

"She's a transfer student, isn't she?" David said, pulling Cory back down to the bench.

"Yeah."

"Well, maybe her file hasn't been sent over from her other school yet."

David was smart. Maybe he was right. But Cory didn't really believe it. It was November already. How long did it take to transfer files?

"Is he talking about that weird blond girl again?" Arnie boomed, leaning over David to shout right in Cory's face. "What have you been doin' to her?" he leered. "Must be pretty good or you wouldn't be missing practice so much." Arnie laughed as if he had just said the funniest thing ever spoken.

Cory just shook his head wearily. He realized he must seem pretty weird to his two friends. He seemed pretty weird to himself.

He'd never been haunted by someone this way before. He'd never had anything that he couldn't shut out of his mind, that he couldn't force himself to stop thinking about. He had always been in control of his thoughts. And now . . . now . . .

Was he out of control?

"See you guys later," he said, and quickly headed the other way down the row so they couldn't pull him back. The crowd groaned, then groaned again. The small contingent of Westerville fans across the floor was cheering wildly.

It looked like a bad night for the Cougars. A bad

night for everyone, Cory thought. He had searched the bleachers row by row for Anna. But she wasn't there.

He climbed into his car, shivering against the chill. After three tries he got it started. He drove around aimlessly for a while, heading down Park Drive, then across Hawthorne to Mill Road. The streets were empty. Most houses were already dark. He turned on the radio, but no one was playing any music he liked, so he clicked it off.

He realized he was very tired. He hadn't slept well all week. He spun the car around and headed for home.

He was asleep when the ringing phone woke him. He squinted at his alarm clock. It was one-thirty in the morning.

His hand knocked the receiver off the phone. He fumbled around until he grabbed it up. "Hello?"

"Stay away from Anna."

"What?" The voice on the other end was a hoarse whisper, so quiet he could barely make out the words.

"Stay away from Anna," the strange voice whispered slowly and distinctly, each word filled with menace. "She's dead. She's a dead girl. Stay away from her—or you'll be next!"

chapter

9

*C*ory suddenly felt very cold. He climbed out of bed and walked in darkness over to his bedroom window. He checked to make sure the window was closed. Then he reached down and felt the radiator. Heat was coming up full blast. He stood there for a long while trying to get rid of the chill, staring out at the silent stillness of his backyard lit only by a pale half moon.

The voice on the phone still whispered in his ears. Cory reached up and pulled his black curls hard, trying to make the harsh whispers disappear, trying to make the threatening words stop repeating in his mind. It didn't work.

Realizing his chill came from the inside, Cory stepped away from the radiator and, tripping over a pair of sneakers he had left in the center of the room, made his way back to bed.

Someone had threatened his life. Someone knew where he lived. Someone knew how to reach him.

Someone knew him and knew he was interested in Anna.

Someone wanted to make sure he stayed away from Anna. But who?

Was it one of his friends playing a joke?

No. This was no joke. This was for real. The whispers were filled with true menace, true hatred. The threat was sincere.

Stay away from Anna—or you'll be dead too.

Who was it? The strange, puffy-cheeked young man who answered the Corwins' door? Maybe. It was hard to tell from whispers, hard to tell if it was a man or a woman.

Cory closed his eyes tight and tried to drive the whispers from his mind. He felt a little warmer now, but he was still far from sleep. He turned onto his side, then slid over onto his other side, then tried sleeping on his stomach.

For some reason he found himself thinking about the strange neighbor who had stopped him that night on Fear Street. He had been thinking about that man all week, picturing his worn gray slicker, his stubbled face, the menacing way he had stared at Cory. He said he was a neighbor, but why was he directly outside the Corwins' house so late at night? He had claimed to be walking his dog. But Cory had seen no dog. And why had the man warned Cory to stay away from the Corwins? Was he warning Cory—or threatening him?

Cory forced the man's face out of his mind. He decided to think about Anna instead—those clear blue eyes as bright as a doll's, the dramatically red lips on that pale ivory skin. He remembered the dream where she was kissing him again and again.

The phone rang.

He was still wide awake, but it startled him, making him jump straight out of bed. He picked up the receiver at the beginning of the second ring. "Hello?" The word came out choked and dry.

"Cory—is that you?" A tiny voice, very faint.

"Yes." His heart was pounding so hard, he could barely get the word out.

"Can you help me, Cory?"

He had spoken to her only once, but he recognized her soft, almost childlike voice.

"It's me. Anna. Anna Corwin."

"I know," he said. Then he felt terribly foolish. How would he know that she would be the one calling him in the middle of the night—unless he had been thinking of nothing but her for weeks?

"I need you to help me," she said, speaking rapidly, her voice just above a whisper. "I don't know anyone else. You're the only one I've talked to. Can you help me?"

She sounded so frightened, so desperately frightened. "Well . . ." Why was he hesitating? Was it because of the first whispered call telling him to stay away from her?

"Please—come quickly," she pleaded. "Meet me on the corner of Fear Street, just past my house."

She sounded frightened. But her tiny, breathy voice also made her sound very sexy. The chill Cory felt now wasn't entirely fear. It was mixed with excitement. He looked across the room at his alarm clock. It was one thirty-seven. Was he *really* seriously considering sneaking out and meeting this strange, frightened girl on Fear Street in the middle of the night?

"Please, Cory," she whispered, now more enticing than frightened. "I need you."

"Okay," he said, not recognizing his own voice, not sure it was him saying the word.

"Hurry," she whispered, and the line clicked off.

He listened to the silent phone for a few seconds, trying to figure out if he was awake or dreaming this. Had Anna Corwin really just called and begged him to meet her? He had been thinking about her, searching for her all week. Was it possible that she had been thinking about him at the same time?

The idea was more than a little exciting. But why had she sounded so frightened, so frantic for him to come at once? And why did she want him to meet her out on the street?

The street.

Fear Street.

Cory had started to pull on his jeans, but he stopped as he remembered where Anna lived, where she wanted to meet.

"I'm sixteen years old," he told himself. "I'm not a child. There's no reason for me to be afraid of a silly street." But he had to admit that the idea of waiting alone for someone on Fear Street in the middle of the night was pretty frightening.

He suddenly remembered another Fear Street story in the newspaper, this one from the previous spring. Two cars going in opposite directions on Fear Street late at night had collided head-on. A Fear Street resident heard the crash, ran out in his pajamas, saw that both cars were filled with badly injured people. Some of them were unconscious. Some were pinned inside the crushed cars.

He ran back to his house and called the police. The police arrived less than ten minutes later. They found the cars crushed together in the middle of the street. But both cars were empty. There was dark blood on the seats and blood on the street. But all the passengers had disappeared without a trace.

No sign of them was ever found. Six people, six injured people, who had been trapped inside two cars, vanished in less than ten minutes. . . .

Cory finished getting dressed. He knew he had no choice. He had to go. He had to go to her. She needed him.

Sneaking down the steps to the front hallway, he tripped in the darkness and nearly fell. He grabbed the banister and steadied himself, hoping his parents hadn't heard. Taking a deep breath, he continued down the stairs. He groped around until he found the car keys on the counter in the entranceway. Then he silently let himself out of the house.

He zipped his down jacket against the cold and jogged to the car. He put the car in neutral and let it glide down the drive. Then he started it in the street as far from the house as he could get it. "I'm getting pretty good at sneaking around," he told himself. "But why am I doing this?"

Because Anna's in trouble.

He turned down Mill Road and headed south toward

Fear Street. Clouds had covered the moon, and the streetlamps cast only dim light on this narrow, old street. He put on the brights just in time to see a large gray animal scamper out onto the highway.

Whump.

There wasn't time to slow down. A single bump told him he had run over it. He looked in the rearview mirror but couldn't see anything. He slowed for a few seconds, then decided to keep going. Nothing he could do about it now.

He suddenly felt sick. What was it anyway? A raccoon? A badger? It was too big to be a rabbit. It might have been an opossum. He wondered if it was stuck to his tire. Yuck. He forced himself to think about Anna.

There were no other cars on Mill Road. He passed a few trucks going the other way, their headlights causing him to squint and look away.

A swirling wind seemed to come up the moment he turned onto Fear Street. The wind pressed against the front of the car. The car held back, as if it didn't want to go here.

The inside of the windshield had steamed up, and he struggled to see. He slowed down as he passed Simon Fear's burned-out mansion. Bare trees rattled and creaked in the wind, their low branches scraping at one another.

He stopped and wiped the windshield with a rag he found in the glove compartment. Now the glass was smeared, but he could see a little better.

He passed the Corwins' house. It was completely

dark. He stopped and stared at it, looking for any sign of life. But there was none.

Had the call been someone playing a joke? Had he driven here for nothing?

No. It was Anna. He recognized her voice. And she sounded too frightened for it to be a joke.

He pulled to the curb at the corner. The wind rushed through the trees. Leaves swirled and scattered over the street. He turned off the lights but left the engine running.

"Maybe I should get out of the car," he told himself. "She might not be able to find me if I stay in here."

But he remembered his last visit to Fear Street, the strange neighbor, the animal howls, and he decided to wait inside the car. He switched off the engine. Then he switched it on again. "I'll play the radio. At least it will drown out the dreadful wailing of the wind." But then he remembered it might drain the battery. He didn't want to be stuck at two in the morning on Fear Street with a car that wouldn't start. He turned the engine off again.

The passenger door swung open.

He started to scream.

chapter

10

"*A*nna!"

"Hi, Cory," she whispered shyly, sliding next to him on the front seat. She was wrapped in an old-fashioned lacy gray shawl. Her hair was wild and unbrushed, and her blue eyes sparkled with excitement in the glimmer of light inside the car. Then she pulled the car door closed and the light faded.

"You frightened me," he said, turning to look at her.

She gave him an odd smile, almost a devilish smile. Or was it just the dim light? He couldn't see her very well.

"Why did you call me? What's the matter?"

She slid closer. She was almost touching him. The wind shifted directions. Leaves blew up against the car windows, making it even darker.

"Cory, you're the only one who can help me," she said, her voice barely above a whisper. She was trembling slightly, as if she were holding back her fear, struggling to keep herself together. "You're the only one who talks to me."

"Where've you been all week?" he blurted out. "I looked for you."

She seemed surprised. She turned and looked to the rear window. It was entirely steamed up. She rubbed the side window next to her with her hand, making a clear peephole.

"Were you sick? Are you okay?" Cory asked.

She smiled at him again.

"I—I was at your house before," he said. "I wanted to talk to you." He realized he must sound crazy to her. The words just poured out. He didn't seem to have any control over what he was saying.

He was so glad to see her, so excited. It was exciting that she had called him, that he had come to her in the middle of the night, that they were having this secret meeting. But what was it all about? Why wasn't she answering any of his questions?

"Are you in trouble?" he asked. "Is there anything I can do? I was thinking about you this week. Actually, I've been thinking about you ever since that day in the lunchroom."

The lunchroom. Why did he have to bring that horrible occasion up? How embarrassing!

"Really?" she said. "I was thinking about you too." She peered out through the small circle she had made on the window.

"Is someone following you?" he asked. "Is someone out there?"

She shook her head. "I don't know."

"Your family said—they told me you were—" Oh, no! Here he was, blurting it out. Why couldn't he control himself? Why was he talking so crazily?

He hated being so out of control. As a gymnast, he practiced keeping every muscle in control. Now he couldn't even control his mouth!

"I—I just need to know if you're real!" he heard himself saying.

The words seemed to surprise her. A smile slowly spread over her face, a sly smile. "I'm real," she whispered, staring into his eyes. "I'll show you."

She reached both hands up suddenly and grabbed the back of his head. Her hands were hot despite the cold of the night. She pulled his face down to hers and pushed her lips against his.

Her lips were soft and warm. Her mouth opened a little, then closed. She kissed him harder, still holding his head.

He struggled to breathe. She pressed harder, uttering a soft sigh. It was the most exciting kiss, more exciting than in any dream he had ever had. He wanted it to last forever. It appeared that it just might.

She kissed him harder. He was startled by how needy she seemed. She gripped the back of his neck and pressed her lips even closer.

Cory couldn't believe how lucky he was. "Is this really happening to me?" he asked himself. He tried to slip his arms around her, but there was no room to move from behind the steering wheel.

She kissed him, pushing her lips at his, until the kiss really hurt. Then she pulled her mouth away from his.

She slid her warm lips across his cheek and up to his ear. He felt her warm, steady breath against his cheek.

She whispered something. "You're all mine now."

Is that what it was? Did he hear her correctly?

You're all mine now?

No. That couldn't be it. He didn't hear it.

"Do you believe I'm real now?" she asked, her hands still on the back of his neck.

He tried to reply, but no sound came out.

She laughed, a surprisingly loud laugh that startled them both. They had both been so quiet up till now.

The wind shifted again. Large brown maple leaves blew hard against the windshield as if trying to break in. Somewhere nearby an animal howled.

She let go of him and settled back in the seat, a pleased expression on her face. He could still feel her lips on his, still taste her, still feel the pressure of her face against his.

They didn't say anything for what seemed a long, long while. Finally he broke the silence. "Why did you call me, Anna?"

He didn't really want her to answer. What he wanted was for her to kiss him again like that. And again. And again.

"You sounded so frightened," he said, reaching for her hand but not finding it.

She smiled at him, this time a guilty smile. "I just wanted to see if you'd come," she said. She looked away. She started rubbing a fresh peephole in the window.

"You—you weren't in trouble?"

She didn't look at him. "I knew you'd come," she said. "I just knew it."

He stared at the back of her head, at her golden hair which fell in long tangles over the gray shawl.

He wanted to kiss her again. He wanted to wrap his arms around her. He wanted to feel her hands on the back of his neck again. He reached out and put a hand on her shoulder. "That's why you called? You just wanted me to come here?"

She turned around, her face expressionless. She looked at him but didn't say anything.

"When I was at your house, a guy answered the door." He had to ask her about it. He just had to. He knew she was real now. So why did her family say she was dead?

"My brother. Brad," she answered, still expressionless. She stared straight ahead at the clouded windshield.

"When I asked for you, he got real upset. He said you didn't live there."

"Brad'll say anything," she whispered, still staring straight ahead at the fogged windshield.

"But he—"

"Please don't make me tell you about Brad. He— he's crazy. Don't make me say any more. Just stay out of his way. He—he can be *dangerous*." Her whole body shook when she said that word.

"He told me you were dead!" Cory blurted out.

For a brief second her eyes grew wide with surprise. Then she pulled the door handle, pushed open the door, and jumped out of the car.

Cory made a grab for her. But she was already gone.

He threw open his door and climbed out. The wind blew a clump of leaves onto the legs of his jeans. "Anna!" he called to her. But he knew he hadn't shouted loudly enough to be heard over the wind.

He started to run after her, but she had disappeared into the darkness. "Anna!" he called one more time. But she was gone.

The wind seemed to grow stronger. The tree limbs above his head rattled like bones as the dry leaves circled and spun at his feet.

He tasted blood on his lips. He was filled with longing, longing to understand her, longing to know why she had run away, why she wouldn't answer his questions, why she was so terrified of her brother, longing for more kisses.

He was only a few feet from the car when something big and powerful leapt onto his shoulders from behind.

chapter

11

"*C*ory—wake up! Come on!"

"Huh?"

"Wake up! Get out of bed! Do I have to get a crane to pull you up?"

"Huh?"

"I've been trying to wake you for ten minutes. What's your problem? Didn't you sleep last night?" His mother grabbed his shoulder and started to shake him.

"*Ow!*" The shoulder throbbed with pain. He jerked it away from her. It was all starting to come back to him. His shoulder hurt because the gigantic dog had jumped on it.

"Cory—come on. You've got a gymnastics meet in two hours. You'd better wake up." His mother was more amused than annoyed. She'd never had this much trouble waking him before.

Of course, he had never spent half the night on Fear Street before. He thought of Anna's kiss.

"What are you smiling about? Cory—you're acting downright weird this morning."

"Sorry, Mom. G'morning." He tried to clear his brain. He smiled at her, only his mouth wouldn't cooperate and it came out all crooked. He tried to look normal. He didn't want her to ask a million questions. If only his back and shoulders weren't killing him.

"What day is it?"

"Saturday," she said, turning to leave.

"Saturday? The meet against Farmingville is today!"

"Didn't I just say that, or am I losing my mind too?"

He sat up in bed with a loud groan. She turned around and looked at him. "Hurry downstairs before your breakfast gets cold."

"What's for breakfast?"

"Cornflakes."

They both laughed. It was one of their favorite jokes.

After she left, he carefully pulled off his pajama top and surveyed the damage to his shoulders. They were just badly scratched. That huge Doberman, Voltaire, had pounced on him as if he were a mouse.

The whole scene with all its horror replayed itself in his mind. He heard the low growls again, felt the dog's hot breath on the back of his head, and then felt the jolt of the giant paws bearing down on his shoulders, pushing him to the ground, pinning him down, the dog's massive jaws snapping loudly as it snarled over him.

It seemed to him he was down on the ground for hours before the strange neighbor in the gray slicker had arrived. "Get down, Voltaire. Sit, boy," he had said calmly, with no emotion at all. The dog obeyed immediately, backing away, silent except for its heavy, excited panting. "You back again, son?"

The guy didn't even apologize. He just stared at Cory suspiciously as Cory slowly, painfully, pulled himself to his feet with a loud groan.

"Visiting the Corwins, were you?" the man asked, petting the Doberman's slender black head as if to congratulate him on a job well done.

"I—uh . . . I was just leaving," Cory stammered, his heart heaving in his chest, his shoulders aching, his head spinning.

"Most folks don't come around Fear Street in the middle of the night," the man said, his expression as unrevealing as ever. It sounded like a threat to Cory.

Cory didn't reply. Somehow he managed to climb into his car, start the engine, and drive away. The man and dog stood watching until Cory was out of sight.

What was going on here? Cory wondered. Why was that weird guy always there when Cory parked near the Corwins' house? Had he been watching for Cory? Was he really a neighbor? Was he spying on Anna?

It's her crazy brother Brad wearing a disguise!

"Get real!" he had scolded himself.

But who was he?

Now it was the next morning, and he was less than two hours away from the Farmingville meet. He looked at his scratched-up shoulders in the mirror. How was he going to explain them to Coach Welner? How was he ever going to get up on the rings? He swung his arms around, testing them. Not too bad. Maybe he could work out the ache. Maybe they'd be flexible enough to perform.

He got dressed quickly, pulling on a clean pair of jeans and a fresh sweatshirt, and hurried down to breakfast. He decided to get to the gym early and work out, do some stretching exercises. He'd be fine.

He thought of Anna. How soft she was, how warm. At least he had proven that she was alive. Wow! Was she alive!

Yeah. He'd be fine, Cory decided. He'd be perfectly fine.

Disgustedly, Cory tossed a towel over his shoulder. He started pacing behind the team bench and bumped right into Lisa. "Ow!" she cried, rubbing her shoulder. "Watch where you're going."

"Hey—what are you doing here? There's a meet going on," Cory said.

"Really? How would *you* know?" she cracked.

"Give me a break. Did you come here just to insult me?" Cory asked glumly. He picked up his pace.

She hurried to catch up with him. "No. Sorry. It just slipped out." She put a hand on his shoulder to stop him, but he pulled away in pain. "What's the matter?"

"I—uh—strained it, I guess." He didn't have the energy to tell her the truth. He wouldn't know where to begin. "You were watching the meet?"

"No. Not really. I got here just in time to see your bar routine."

"It wasn't a bar routine. It was a clown act," Cory said with genuine sadness.

"Sorry," she said. She started to pat his shoulder again but quickly thought better of it. "I came to tell you something. Something I think you'll be interested in." She looked tense. She was biting her lower lip.

"Can it wait till after? Coach is gonna—"

"It's about Anna Corwin," she said.

"Tell me," he said, tossing the towel to the floor.

She frowned. She took both his hands and pulled him to the side of the gym. "We were at my cousin's house last night," she told him, leaning back against the tile wall.

"Which cousin?"

"What does it matter? You don't know any of my cousins."

"Oh. Right."

"My cousin had a friend over, a girl who goes to Melrose. And I was talking to her, and I asked her if she knew Anna Corwin because Anna used to go to Melrose before she transferred here."

"Yeah. And?"

"Well, when I asked her about Anna, the girl got this funny look on her face. She actually went pale."

"Why?" Cory asked impatiently. "What did she tell you?"

"Well, you're not going to believe this. She said that Anna *had* been in her class—but that Anna was dead."

chapter

12

Cory's face filled with surprise, and then anger. "That's not funny, Lisa. Why'd you pull me away from the meet to tell me such a stupid—"

He started to go back, but she shoved him back against the wall. *"Owwch!"* His shoulders throbbed with pain.

"Oh. Sorry. Just let me finish. It isn't a joke. It was a terrible tragedy, my cousin's friend said. There were rumors about Anna Corwin all over her school. No one was sure what really happened. The story was that Anna had fallen down the basement stairs in her house. She died instantly in the fall."

"But that's impossible," Cory said weakly. He thought of their kiss the night before. He felt Anna's lips pressing so hard against his. "Totally impossible."

"My cousin's friend swore that it was true," Lisa told him. "It happened over the summer vacation, and people were still talking about it in the fall."

"No way," Cory said, bending over to retrieve the towel. "I don't believe it. I just don't."

"There's an easy way to prove it," Lisa said. "Get dressed. Let's go do some investigating."

"Are you kidding? In the middle of the meet?" He glanced nervously over to the coach. Coach Welner was unhappily engrossed in Arnie's bar routine.

"You're finished anyway, aren't you?" Lisa asked impatiently.

"Yeah. In more ways than one," Cory said glumly, suddenly remembering the pathetic performance he had just given. "But if Coach catches me ducking out in the middle . . ."

He changed his mind. He knew he had no choice. He had to find out the truth about Anna—right away. "Okay. Meet you in the parking lot," he said.

Making sure that Coach Welner was still watching Arnie's performance on the bar, Cory slipped out of the door and into the locker room, where he changed into his street clothes as quickly as he could.

This story about Anna couldn't be true.

She couldn't be dead. She *couldn't!*

That wasn't a ghost he had kissed—*was* it?

He suddenly remembered the frightened look on her face the first time he had ever talked to her, when he had mentioned ghosts on Fear Street.

No. Get real. There was no such thing as ghosts. The girl who had kissed him with such heat, such feeling, had to be alive!

A few minutes later he had sneaked out of the building and was with Lisa in her car, heading toward the Shadyside public library. A light snow had fallen during the afternoon, covering the trees, making them look ghostlike in the gray light of evening.

"What's at the library?" he asked her, breaking a long silence.

"The computer lab. They have all the local papers from all over the state on LexisNexis there. I use this room a lot to do research for articles I write for the *Spectator.*"

They rode the rest of the way in silence.

At the library Lisa looked for the Melrose newspapers from four and five months before.

About twenty minutes later she found what they were looking for. It was a newspaper article from the previous spring. Cory stared at the black type of the headline on the screen.

ANNA CORWIN, MELROSE SOPHOMORE,
DIES IN ACCIDENT

The words to the story all blurred in Cory's eyes. But there was a photograph that he couldn't stop staring at. The photo was very unclear. The reproduction was too light, all in grays, as if the girl had been a ghost to begin with.

It's Anna, he thought. Those eyes. The blond hair. It's Anna. He squinted into the computer, trying, to make the gray photo clearer.

"But—how—I mean—how can you explain this?" he managed to say, still staring into the screen, his thoughts swirling crazily through his mind, thoughts of Anna, of talking to her, of touching her.

"I can't explain it," Lisa said softly. "I don't know

what to say."

He stared at the gray photograph and then back at the bold headline.

The question repeated endlessly in his mind . . .

How could Anna Corwin be dead?

How could Anna Corwin be dead?

He felt her lips again, pressing so hard against his, pressing, harder, harder until his lips bled.

How could Anna Corwin be dead?

That night Cory was too restless to do anything. He tried catching up on some of his homework, but he couldn't concentrate. At eight-thirty he sneaked out of the house and drove around town for a while. There were small patches of white along the sides of the roads and dotting the lawns, remnants of the light snowfall earlier in the day.

He drove around aimlessly, making the same circle through North Hills, down past the high school, across Canyon Road, and then back up again. But he knew all along where he would end up.

On Fear Street.

He parked at the curb in front of the Corwins' yard and stared up at the rambling house. The sky above it was red, casting down an eerie light that made the old house look unreal, like the set of a horror movie.

The inside of the house was completely dark, as usual. A shutter on the side banged noisily in the wind. A dim light went on in an upstairs window. Cory stared at it, unable to see anyone moving inside, and in a minute or so the light flickered out.

He heard a noise behind him, a loud bark. In the

rearview mirror he saw the large black Doberman bearing down on the car, galloping like a horse across the dark street. The neighbor in the gray sticker was close behind.

There he is again, Cory thought. Do he and the dog prowl Fear Street all night? Are they ghosts too?

The Ghostly Guards, he thought. They've been assigned to keep people from discovering the truth about Fear Street—from discovering that everyone who lives on Fear Street is DEAD!

He shook his head hard, trying to shake away the ridiculous thoughts. Then he frantically started the engine and pressed his foot all the way down on the gas pedal. In the rearview mirror he could see the man and the dog pull up short, startled by his fast getaway.

He drove straight home and hurried up to bed. He fell asleep quickly and dreamed about a gymnastics meet. He was up on the rings and realized he didn't know how to get down. Everyone was staring at him, waiting for him to move. But he just couldn't remember how to do it.

He was awakened by someone touching his face.

He sat up in bed, grateful that the dream was interrupted. The hand slid down his cheek again. He blinked himself awake.

Anna!

She was on his bed. She sat beside him, her blue eyes staring down into his.

"What are you doing here? How did you get in?" he asked, his voice a hoarse whisper still filled with sleep.

"Take care of me, Cory. Please," she pleaded,

looking frightened and forlorn. She touched his cheek again. She brushed her lips against his forehead.

"Anna—"

She pressed her face against his.

He couldn't believe this was happening. She was alone with him. In his bedroom. He wanted another kiss. He desperately wanted another kiss like the one in the car.

"Anna—" He reached up for her. He wanted to pull her down on top of him.

She smiled at him. Her soft hair brushed over his face.

"Anna—why did your family say you were dead?"

She didn't seem at all surprised or upset by the question. "I *am* dead," she whispered in his ear. "I *am* dead, Cory. But you can still take care of me."

"What do you mean?" He suddenly felt very frightened. She looked very ghostly now, pale and transparent. Her eyes burned into his. They weren't friendly eyes. They were menacing eyes, evil eyes.

"What do you mean?" he repeated, unable to keep the fear from his voice.

"You can die too," she whispered. "Then we can be together.

"No!" he cried, pushing her away, "No—I don't want to!"

The phone was ringing.

He sat up and looked around.

No Anna. It had been a dream. It had all been a dream.

But it had seemed so real.

The phone was real. He looked at his desk clock. It was a little after midnight. He grabbed up the receiver.

"Hello, Cory?" A whispered voice. Anna's voice.

"Hi, Anna," he whispered back.

"Cory—come quickly. Please! You've got to come! Please! But don't park by my house! I'll meet you in front of that burned-out old mansion. Hurry, Cory! You're the only one I can turn to!"

chapter

13

*H*e held on to the phone long after she had hung up. He needed to know that it was real, that he wasn't dreaming this too.

Yes. She had really called him. She was real. She was alive.

Should he go? Did he have a choice?

He thought of her sitting so close to him in the car, pressing her face against his, kissing him, kissing him, kissing him.

Of *course* he had to go!

She needed him.

And he needed . . . to ask her all the questions that were in his mind, to find out the truth about her once and for all.

He got dressed in seconds, turned off the desk lamp, and started to sneak silently down the stairs. He was halfway down when his parents' bedroom door opened, and his father lumbered out into the dark hallway. "Cory—is that you?"

He had to answer. If he didn't, his dad would think it was a burglar. "Yeah, Dad. It's me," he whispered.

"What's the matter? What are you doing?"

Think fast, Cory. Think fast. "Uh . . . I'm just going down for a snack. I woke up 'cause I was hungry."

His father grunted, accepting the story. "Thought I heard the phone ring," he said, yawning.

"Yeah. It was a wrong number," Cory said.

He waited until he heard his father go back in and close the bedroom door. He waited another minute or two. Then he crept silently down the rest of the stairs and out the front door.

It was even colder than the first night he had sneaked out, but there was no wind at all. The ground felt hard and frosty beneath his sneakers. The moon was hidden behind thick clouds. Again, he let the car roll down the drive, then started it on the street.

Mill Road was as dark and empty as before. Cory stared at the curving white line in the center of the narrow road and thought about Anna.

Was she really in trouble this time? She sounded very frightened, very frantic. What could the problem be? Was she afraid to tell him?

Or did she just want to see him? If so, why could she see him only in the middle of the night? And why couldn't he park near her house? Why did she have to meet him in front of Simon Fear's creepy old mansion?

He thought of the disturbing dream he had just had about her. And the photo in the newspaper article flashed into his mind. He forced himself not to think about that. He wanted to kiss her again. And again.

This was so exciting!

He turned onto Fear Street and stopped in front of the burned-out mansion. Across the street the cemetery lay dark and still. He turned off the headlights. The blackness enveloped him. He couldn't see a thing. He suddenly felt as if the blackness had walled him off from the rest of the world, as if he had entered a black tunnel, an endless black tunnel, a tunnel leading to . . .

He turned around to look out the back window for her. No sign of her. Nothing moved. The trees, black shadows against the blacker sky, could have been painted on a backdrop.

He rolled down the window and breathed the frigid air. He looked for her in the rearview mirror. She still wasn't coming. He reached for the door handle to get out of the car. But remembering the huge Doberman, he decided against it.

It was too cold with the window down. He rolled it back up. Where was she? He held his wrist up to check the time, but he had forgotten to put on his watch. He turned again and peered out the back window. Only blackness.

Despite the cold, his palms were hot and sweaty. He coughed. His throat felt tight and dry. He couldn't sit still any longer. He was too nervous.

He pushed open the door and climbed out. He closed the door quickly so no one could see the light. He listened for the neighbor and his vicious four-legged companion. The Ghostly Guards. Silence.

"This must be what it's like on the moon," he told

himself. So quiet. So still. So . . . unreal. The insistent theme music from *The Twilight Zone* ran through his mind.

Where was she?

He started to walk down the long block toward her house. The air was cold and wet, so wet it seemed to cling to him as he walked. He stopped at the edge of her driveway and looked up at the old house.

Dark. Completely dark.

Or was it? Was that a sliver of light escaping from beneath a second-story window blind?

Someone was awake in there. Was it Anna?

Was she waiting for the right moment to sneak out and come down to him? Was someone keeping her from making her escape?

Brad.

Crazy Brad.

He shuddered as a chill ran through his body. He decided to go back and wait in the car. The street was so dark, he couldn't see more than a few feet in front of him. The only sounds were his footsteps as he trudged over the gravelly road. Finally he climbed into the car and closed the door. It wasn't much warmer inside. He slid down low in the seat, pulling his head down into his jacket, trying to warm up.

Where was she?

He stared at the windshield, watching it frost up from his breath.

Was he shivering from the cold? Or from the fact that he was starting to worry about her?

Maybe something terrible had happened to her.

Maybe she had called him because she knew she was in danger—and he hadn't come soon enough.

Staring at the opaque layers of steam on the windshield, Cory's ideas grew wilder and wilder. Maybe Brad was holding Anna prisoner in that house. She had said that Brad was dangerous. That was the very word she had used. *Dangerous.* Maybe she wanted Cory to help her escape from Brad. Only Brad had found out about her plan, and he had—he had—what?

He pushed open the door and jumped out. He looked back down the block toward her house. She wasn't coming. His breath was forming curtains of smoke in front of him. He realized he was breathing very rapidly, and his heart was pounding.

Where was she?

He had no choice. He had to go to her house. He had to make sure she was okay.

She had called him for help, and all he had done was sit in his car trying to stay warm. Some help.

He began jogging to her house, his sneakers thudding loudly over the hard ground, the only sound beside his gasping breaths. He turned up the gravel drive and picked up speed. Looking up, he saw the thin sliver of light in the upstairs bedroom.

The ground tilted and swayed. He forced himself to keep jogging steadily. Up on the porch now. Then he was ringing the bell, forgetting that it was broken. Then he was knocking on the door, first a normal knock, then, when no one answered, as hard as he could.

Where was she?

What were they doing to her?

The door swung open. Brad, looking sleepy and puffy-eyed, stepped quickly out onto the porch, nearly knocking Cory over backward. His little eyes opened briefly with surprise, then narrowed as anger spread over his pink face.

"You—" he said, and turned his face as if to spit.

Cory tried to say something, but he was too out of breath.

"What do you want now?" Brad asked, leaning menacingly over Cory. "What are you doing here?"

"Anna called me—" Cory managed to get out.

Brad's face filled with rage. He reached out and grabbed the front of Cory's jacket. "Are you trying to torture me?" he screamed. "Is this some kind of cruel prank?"

Cory tried to pull away, but Brad's grip was surprisingly strong. "Wait. I—"

"I told you—" Brad screamed at the top of his lungs, "ANNA IS DEAD! ANNA IS DEAD! Why can't you believe me?"

He was pulling Cory's jacket so hard, Cory was having trouble breathing. In a desperate attempt to free himself, Cory brought both hands up and smashed them down against Brad's forearms.

Brad let go. Cory started to back away.

This seemed to enrage Brad even more. He grabbed Cory by the jacket front again and started dragging him. He pulled him through the open front door and into the house. "Now I'm going to get rid of you once and for all," Brad said.

chapter

14

*T*his isn't happening to me, Cory told himself. This is just another bad dream. Wake up now, Cory. Wake up.

He didn't wake up. He was already awake. This was no dream.

Brad pulled him into the living room. The house felt hot and steamy. The air smelled stale. A small fire was going in the fireplace against the far wall. There were no other lights. Shadows twisted on the dark walls. The fire crackled loudly, startling Cory.

Brad laughed. He was really enjoying Cory's fear.

He loosened his grip on Cory's jacket. Cory took a step back. Brad's stud earring sparkled in the firelight. His eyes grew watery from laughing. "You're really scared of me—aren't you?" he demanded, wiping tears from his eyes.

Cory didn't reply. He stared back at the odd young man, trying to figure out how to escape if Brad attacked again. But he was too frightened to think clearly.

"Get out of here," Brad growled. "I'm letting you go. But don't ever come back."

Cory hesitated for a second. He wasn't sure he had heard right. Then he ran past Brad and out of the house. The door slammed hard behind him.

The shock of the cold air revived him quickly. He stopped halfway down the driveway, turned, and looked up to the second-floor window. The blind had been raised and light poured out into the surrounding darkness.

A figure stood in the window looking down on him.

"Anna!" he called, cupping his hands around his mouth. "Anna—is that you?" He waved frantically to her.

The figure in the window pulled down the blind.

The front yard returned to total darkness.

"How far can you spit that?"

"What? This peach pit?" Arnie held up the red pit between his finger and his thumb.

"Yeah. How far?" David asked, his expression serious, as if he were making a scientific survey.

"I can spit it into that wastebasket," Arnie said, pointing to a green wastebasket on the other side of the lunchroom, at least a hundred feet away. "Easy."

"You're crazy," David said. "You'll never make it."

"No problem," Arnie insisted. "In fact, it's too easy. Tell you what. See that kid with the red hair, sort of looks like you? I'll ricochet it off that kid's head and into the wastebasket. Just to make it hard."

"No way," David said, shaking his head. "You can't spit it half that far. What do you think, Brooks?"

"What?" Cory looked up from his ham sandwich.

"Think he can do it?"

Cory shrugged his shoulders. "Sorry. I was thinking about something else." He was thinking about Anna, of course. He'd been trying to phone her for two days. No one had answered the phone.

"Arnie says he can spit the pit into the basket over there," David explained.

"So?" Cory frowned.

"So? Have you lost all interest in sports, Brooks?" David demanded. "Bad enough you've lost your sense of humor. Now you don't care about major-league athletic demonstrations?"

"Why don't you guys grow up?" Cory said wearily. He took a bite of the sandwich, but he felt too tired to chew.

"You're wrecked, man," Arnie said, rolling the peach pit around in his fingers. "What's your problem, anyway?"

"I—I haven't been getting much sleep," Cory told him.

"That blond girl keeping you up late?" Arnie said with an exaggerated leer. "How come you're not sharing any of this with your pals?"

"Leave him alone," David said, turning Arnie around in his chair. "Spit the pit. Five dollars says it doesn't go halfway across the room."

"You're on, man," Arnie said. "That's a bet." He

tossed the peach pit into his mouth and took a deep breath.

Suddenly his eyes popped open wide. He grabbed his neck. His mouth fell open. He gasped for breath.

"Oh, no! He swallowed it! He's choking!" David screamed, leaping up from his chair and frantically pounding Arnie on the back.

Arnie's face turned bright red. He was struggling to breathe, but it was obvious that he couldn't.

"Help! Somebody help!" Cory yelled.

"Oh, my God! He's choking to death!" David, horrified, went white as flour, looked as if he might faint.

"Help—somebody—"

Cory stopped screaming. He stared at Arnie. He realized that Arnie was laughing now. Arnie winked at him. He held up his hand. The peach pit was still inside it. He had never even put it into his mouth.

"Gotcha," Arnie told his two friends, grinning triumphantly. He collapsed on the table in riotous laughter. David quickly revived and joined him, laughing and pounding the table.

Cory stood up and disgustedly threw the rest of his lunch in the trash. "You guys are just sick," he muttered.

"Hey, come on, Brooks," Arnie said, "what's your problem? It's funny, and you know it."

Cory shook his head and went out the door. He wandered around the parking lot for a while. It was bitter cold and he didn't have his jacket, but he didn't notice.

He was trying to convince himself to stop thinking

about Anna, to just erase her from his mind. He knew he'd feel so much better if he could just forget about her and go back to his old life.

Look at me, he thought. I'm totally wrecked. I've had no sleep. My schoolwork is suffering. My gymnastics is suffering. *I'm* suffering! And all because of a girl whose creepy brother keeps telling me she is *dead!*

He *had* to drop her, force her out of his life. He knew that's what he had to do.

But he also knew he couldn't do it.

At least not until he got some answers. About the newspaper clipping. About her brother. About why she had called him and then not shown up . . .

He heard the warning bell ring inside the building. It was almost time for fifth period. Shivering, he felt the cold for the first time and, rubbing his arms to warm them, hurried back into the building.

He and Lisa arrived at their lockers at the same time.

"How's it going?" she asked.

He tilted his hand from side to side to indicate so-so.

"I'm really sorry about Saturday," she said. "I mean, about the gymnastics match, and everything."

He searched her face to see if she was making fun of him, but she looked sincerely sorry.

"There's always another match," he muttered.

"I guess," she said. She was acting strange, he noticed. Awkward. She wasn't teasing him or putting him down the way she had for their entire lives.

"So, how's it going with you?" he asked.

"Okay." She was having trouble with her combination lock. Finally she pulled it open and opened her locker. "Can I ask you something?" Her voice was muffled behind the locker door.

"Sure," he said. It wasn't like Lisa to be so formal. If she had something to ask, she usually just asked it.

"Uh . . . well . . . You know there's the Turnaround Dance here Saturday night. Want to go with me?" She asked it very fast, as if it were all one word. She was still hiding behind the locker door.

Cory was very surprised. He and Lisa had been friends their whole lives. But they'd never gone out on a *date!*

It was a really good idea, he decided quickly. He had to try to forget about Anna. Or at least not think about her all the time. Going out with Lisa would help him. What a good friend Lisa was. She really was there for him when he needed her.

"Sure," he said. "Great!"

Lisa peeked out from behind her locker door. She had a big smile on her face. "I'll pick you up at eight o'clock," she said. She sounded genuinely excited.

Cory smiled back at her. Lisa was certainly acting weird, as if she had a crush on him or something. He glanced past her down the fast-emptying corridor. Was that Anna watching them in the shadows two classrooms down?

Or was he just imagining that it was Anna?

"I've *got* to get her out of my mind," he told himself, feeling genuinely frightened. "Now I'm starting to see her everywhere!"

But, wait. She stepped out of the shadows. She was walking toward them. It *was* Anna.

She walked quickly between them and gave Cory a warm smile. "Hi," she said softly, her eyes revealing that she was happy to see him. She was wearing a white blouse and an old-fashioned flower-patterned jumper. Somehow she looked even more fragile than usual.

"Hi," Cory said. He took a step back. She was standing a little too close to him. He looked at Lisa, who looked very surprised.

"Hi," Lisa said, sticking out her hand to shake hands. "We haven't really met. I'm Lisa. Lisa Blume. You're in my physics class."

"Yes, I know," Anna said, shaking Lisa's hand and giving her a warm smile. "I've noticed you. You're very funny."

"Unfortunately, funny doesn't get you too far in physics," Lisa said, shaking her head. She pulled at her black curls. She seemed nervous. "When did you move to Shadyside?"

"A few weeks ago," Anna told her. "It's hard being a new girl here. It's such a big school. I used to go to Melrose upstate. We had only two hundred students. Cory's about the only new friend I've made here." She smiled at Cory. He could feel himself blushing.

"Lucky girl," Lisa said with her usual sarcasm. She gave Cory a funny look.

"How long have you two known each other?" Anna asked Lisa.

"Too long," Lisa cracked.

Cory didn't join in their laughter. He couldn't take his eyes off Anna. She was so beautiful. And it was so great having a normal conversation with her, seeing her get along so well with Lisa.

Anna suddenly looked upset. "Gee, I hope I didn't interrupt anything," she said to Lisa. "I'm sorry. I heard you ask Cory to the dance. Then I just barged in here between you two and—"

"No. Don't be silly," Lisa said. She glanced at her watch. "Oh. The bell's gonna ring. I promised I'd be early today. I've gotta run." She picked up her bookbag and slammed her locker shut. "Bye, Cory! Nice meeting you, Anna!" she shouted as she ran down the hallway.

As soon as Lisa disappeared around the corner, Anna grabbed Cory's hand and squeezed it tightly. "Remember Friday night?" she whispered into his ear, standing on tiptoe to reach it.

Yes, he remembered Friday night. But with her standing so close to him holding his hand, he completely forgot everything else he ever knew.

"Yeah," he said. Brilliant reply, Cory. Very impressive.

She brushed his ear with her lips and whispered something else. He couldn't quite make out what it was. It sounded like "You're all mine now." But that couldn't be it.

"Hey, Anna—" he started. "We've got to talk. I've got to ask you about—"

But she covered his mouth with her hand. Then she replaced the hand with her lips and kissed him. The kiss seemed to last forever. Cory had to struggle to breathe. They were finally interrupted by someone whistling at them.

Anna pulled back. Cory looked up to see who whistled.

The bell rang.

"Bye, Cory," she whispered, giving him a conspiratorial smile, and ran off down the hall.

"No, wait—"

But she was gone. And now he was late for class. He shook his head. He knew he wouldn't hear a word that was said in any of his classes. He'd be thinking about Anna all afternoon.

"Smooth move, ace."

"Huh?"

"You heard me," Lisa said. It was three hours later. School was over for the afternoon. They had met once again at their lockers. "When Mr. Martin stood right in front of you and said, 'Cory, I don't think you've heard a word I said today,' and you said 'What?' Real smooth move."

"Get off my case," Cory snapped. "I just wasn't listening, that's all."

"Guess not." Lisa laughed. "What are you doing now? You got practice?"

"Yeah. I'm still on the team, believe it or not," Cory muttered dispiritedly.

"Well . . . uh . . . do you want to come over after dinner? Maybe study and . . ." She opened her locker and reached inside. "Hey—there's something sticky . . ."

She pulled her hand out. And then she screamed.

Her hand was covered with blood.

"Lisa—what is it?" Cory asked.

A dead cat flopped out of her locker and dropped onto her white sneakers. The locker was splattered with blood. The cat's stomach had been slit open.

Lisa pressed her head against the cool tile wall. "I don't believe this. . . . I don't believe this. . . ." She kept repeating herself, not moving from the wall.

Cory saw something tied around the dead cat's throat. It was a note written on white notebook paper.

He bent down, pulled it off, and read it to himself: "LISA—YOU'RE DEAD TOO."

chapter

15

"*A*nna!"

"Hi, Cory. I waited for you. How was practice?"

He sighed and tossed his bookbag wearily over his shoulder. "Don't ask. I didn't make it to practice."

"Oh." She hurried to keep up with him as he headed down the walk and toward the street. It was five o'clock, and the sky was already dark. A wet wind blew in their faces, gusting around them, making it hard to walk.

But Cory needed fresh air. He needed to move, to use his muscles, to let off some energy. "I had to help Lisa clean her locker," he said. He spun around and looked into Anna's eyes. He wanted to see if she had any idea what he was talking about.

"What is she—an obsessively neat person?" Anna asked, laughing a light musical laugh. "Whoever heard of cleaning out your locker when school has just started?"

She didn't seem to know about the cat. Or else she was a really good actress.

As they cleaned up the mess, Lisa had insisted that Anna had to be the prime suspect. "She heard that we're going to the dance together. She's jealous," Lisa had said, watching the paper towels in her hand soak up the cat's dark red blood.

"Get real. I've never gone out with her," Cory had insisted.

"I saw the way she looked at you," Lisa said. "The way she stood next to you. Very possessive. She did this. I know it."

"That's just stupid." Lisa's accusations were making Cory really angry.

"Go get more paper towels," Lisa said. "Uccch. I think I'm going to be sick. It's a good thing I hate cats."

Now, an hour and a half later, Cory was walking in the wind, explaining to Anna what had happened. "It was a dead cat. Someone had slit open its stomach," he told her. He studied Anna's reaction.

Her mouth formed a small *O* of horror. "No!"

"Someone tied a note around the cat's neck," Cory continued. "It said, 'You're dead too.' "

"How horrible!" Anna cried, raising her hand to her mouth. "Poor Lisa. Who would do such a disgusting thing?"

She seemed genuinely distressed. Cory felt guilty for suspecting her. He knew she hadn't done it.

"Want to go get a Coke or something?" he asked.

"No." She shook her head, her light hair tossing

110

wildly in the strong wind. "Let's just walk. I can't believe that about Lisa. That's so horrible."

"Let's change the subject," he said, trying to brighten up.

"I heard you were the best gymnast at Shadyside last year," she said, obediently changing the subject.

"That was last year," he said quietly.

That was before *you* arrived, he thought.

"All athletes have slumps, don't they?" she asked softly, taking his arm, using him as a shield against the wind.

"Let's change the subject again," he said.

"Maybe we could talk about the Turnaround Dance," she said softly, putting her mouth right up to his ear. It sent a chill down his back.

"What about it?" he asked.

"Wouldn't you rather go with me?" Her voice got tiny and sweet, like a little child begging for candy.

"Well . . . uh . . . yeah . . . I guess."

"Great!"

"But I couldn't do that to Lisa. We've been friends too long and—"

"Oh." She frowned in disappointment, then almost immediately her face brightened again. "Oh, well. Some other time, I guess."

They turned down Park Drive, walking slowly, Anna holding on lightly to his arm, so lightly he could barely feel her touch through his down jacket. It felt great to be walking with her. She was so beautiful. Walking down the tree-lined street, the tall streetlights just coming on to brighten the gray evening, she seemed prettier, calmer, and happier than he had ever seen her.

He felt bad about interrupting this peaceful moment. But he realized he had no choice. There were too many questions he had to ask her, too many things he was eager to know.

"I was at your house again," he started. He could feel her tighten her grip on his arm, as if she expected what was about to come next, as if she expected it— and dreaded it. "Your brother . . . Brad . . . he answered the door again."

"Brad." She mouthed the word without making a sound.

Cory stopped walking and turned to face her. "He seemed very upset, Anna. He grabbed me and pulled me into the house and started to rough me up. He kept saying you were dead."

Her mouth dropped open in shock. She uttered a cry, a squeal of pain and surprise, like a small dog that's been stepped on. "No!"

She slipped off his arm and started to run down the sidewalk, her white moccasins not making a sound.

He wasn't going to let her get away this time. Flinging his bookbag to the ground, he ran after her. He caught her easily, grabbed her arms, and spun her around.

She refused to look at him. "Go away!" she cried, shoving him back. "Go away, Cory. You don't want to get involved."

"I'm already involved!" he told her, refusing to let her go. "I can't stop thinking about you!"

Those words caused her to stop struggling. She

112

stared at him questioningly, as if she didn't believe it, as if she couldn't have heard him correctly. "I'm sorry," she said, her voice a whisper.

As darkness settled, the air grew even colder and the wind picked up. He let go of her arms. She turned and started walking back in the direction of the high school. He followed, walking a few steps behind her. "I have to know the truth," he said. "Why did your brother say that about you?"

"I don't know," she answered without looking back. "I told you he was crazy."

"Someone called me before you did last Friday night and told me not to see you because you were dead, and if I did see you, I'd be dead too. Was that your brother?"

"I don't know," she said. "I really don't know. You've *got* to believe me." She started walking faster. He had to hurry to keep up.

"But why would your brother say a thing like that?" Cory demanded. "Why would he tell people you were dead?"

She spun around, and he almost ran into her. "I don't know! I don't know! I don't know! He's crazy! I told you! He's crazy—and he's very dangerous!" she shouted, tears forming in her eyes. "I really can't talk about it. Don't you understand?"

"Who else lives with you?" Cory asked, deliberately lowering his voice. He didn't want to make her cry, didn't want her to get hysterical. The poor girl obviously had a troubled brother who was making life difficult for her.

"Just my mother," Anna answered, wiping her eyes

with the backs of her hands. "But she isn't very well. It's just the three of us."

They walked on a little in silence, side by side. "Don't listen to Brad," she said finally. "I'm here. I'm here with you. Don't listen to him. Just stay away from him. He mustn't know about . . . about us."

"Sorry for all the questions," he said softly, putting his arm around her shoulder. "I didn't mean to upset you. It's just that I didn't know what to think, and you—you called me Saturday night and then—"

"What? No, Cory. You mean Friday night."

"You called me Saturday night, too, and I came as fast as I could and—"

She turned and stopped him by putting both hands on his chest. She looked very upset. "Someone played a horrible joke on you," she said, her blue eyes burning into his. "I never called you Saturday night."

"Then who—"

"Shhhhh. It's okay," she said, putting her finger to his lips. "Let's not talk anymore." She tilted her head up. He leaned down and started to kiss her.

"No!" she cried suddenly, startling him. She pulled away. She wasn't looking at him. She was looking past him to the tall hedges that bordered the sidewalk. "I've got to go. Don't follow. He's watching me!"

She turned and ran up the street toward the high school. Cory stood helplessly watching her flee for a few seconds. Then he moved quickly to investigate the hedges. He ran around to the other side.

About a hundred yards away someone in a dark fur parka was running at full speed in the other direction along the hedge. Was it Brad?

Could be.

Anna was telling the truth.

Now her crazy brother was spying on them.

"Well, I heard the big news."

"What?" Cory looked up from the new issue of *Sports Illustrated*.

"I heard the big news," his mother repeated. She seemed annoyed that Cory didn't know what she was talking about. "I was just talking to Lisa's mother."

"Yeah?" Cory flipped through till he found the gymnastics article he was looking for. "And what's the big news?"

"About you and Lisa," Mrs. Brooks said impatiently.

"Huh?"

She walked over and stood in front of the couch, forcing him to look up from the magazine. "Am I speaking to Cory Brooks of planet Earth?" she asked.

He rolled his eyes. "Give me a break."

"Well, are you or are you not going out on a date with Lisa?"

"Oh." He suddenly remembered the Turnaround Dance. "Yeah. Yeah, I guess." What was the big deal? Why was his mom smiling like that? Why did she seem so pleased?

"I always knew it would happen," she said, crossing her arms as if hugging herself and going up on tiptoes, then quickly back down, repeating it several times. It was her own peculiar exercise. She always did it instead of standing still.

"What?"

"I always knew the time would come when you and Lisa wouldn't want to be just friends anymore."

"Mom, what planet are *you* from?" Cory asked disgustedly.

"Well, I just think it's nice that you and Lisa—"

"I've got more important things to think about," he said.

"Like what?"

Like Anna, he thought. But he didn't say anything. He just shrugged.

"Like your homework?" she asked.

"Oh. Right. I forgot." He climbed off the couch and started quickly up to his room. "Thanks for reminding me," he called down. "Thanks a bunch."

"Anytime," he heard her say from the kitchen. "Hey, your father and I are going out. So you'll have peace and quiet for studying!"

He sat down at his desk and tried to concentrate on ancient China. But his mind kept wandering. Anna's face kept drifting into his thoughts, taking him away from the fourth Ming dynasty. Again and again he saw the look of terror on her face when she realized that Brad was watching them.

Why was she so afraid of Brad? What hold did he have over her? What was he doing to her?

He realized he hadn't gotten satisfactory answers from her. In fact, he hadn't gotten *any* answers. Anna really seemed too frightened to talk about it.

He decided if he underlined the text, it might help him to concentrate. He opened his desk drawer and began to search for a yellow highlighter. The phone rang.

He stared at it, a heavy feeling forming in the pit of his stomach.

He used to look forward to the phone ringing. Now the sound filled him with dread.

It rang a second time. A third time.

He was alone in the house. He could just let it ring forever. He stared at it, his hand only inches away from the receiver.

Should he answer it or not?

chapter
16

*"H*ello?"

"Hi, Cory."

"David? Hi." He was very relieved to hear David's voice.

"What's happening?"

"Not much. Studying. Reading stuff."

"What are you reading?"

"I'm not sure," Cory told him. They both laughed.

They talked for a while about nothing at all. It was the most relaxed conversation they had had in weeks, probably because Cory was so glad it was David on the phone.

Finally Cory asked, "What's up? Why'd you call?"

"I thought maybe you'd just like to talk," David said, suddenly sounding uncomfortable.

"Okay. So we talked," Cory said, not catching on.

"No. I mean—" David hesitated. "About why you've been so weird lately. Why you've been messing up, you know, cutting practice and stuff. I thought maybe—"

"Nothing to talk about," Cory said sharply.

"I didn't mean to interfere or anything. I just thought—" David sounded really hurt.

"I'm okay," Cory insisted. He really didn't feel like getting into it. He just didn't have the energy. "I've had other things on my mind, I guess."

"You mean the new girl?"

"Well, yeah. . . ."

"She's really cool," David said, his highest compliment. "She's . . . different."

"Yeah," Cory agreed quickly. But he really didn't want to talk about Anna with David. "Listen, I gotta get off."

"Sure you don't want to talk . . . about anything?"

"No. Thanks, David. I'm okay. Really. I'm getting my timing back, I think. I was much better at the meet on Saturday. And—"

"I guess that wasn't you who slipped off the bars a few seconds into your warm-up."

"Anyone can fall, David," Cory said, becoming annoyed. "I just lost my concentration for a second—"

"Lost your concentration! Cory, you've been in a dream world ever since you met Anna. You've been walking around like you fell off the rings and landed on your head!"

"So? What's it to you?" Cory heard himself whine, surprised at his own vehemence.

"Well, I thought I was your friend," David said, sounding as exasperated as Cory.

"Well, friends don't give friends a hard time," Cory said. "See you around, David."

"Not if I see you first," David said.

Normally they would have cracked up over that stupid old line. But this time they both just hung up.

Cory angrily paced back and forth in his room for a while. He couldn't decide whom he was angry at—himself or David. He finally decided he was upset at himself for letting David get him so annoyed.

He slammed his world history text shut. He paced a little while longer. He knew he should be studying, but he just couldn't concentrate. He leaned down on the windowsill and stared out into the night. Across the yard the light in Lisa's room was on. Cory decided to walk over and see how she was doing.

His sneakers slid over the wet grass. He knocked softly on the kitchen door, then a little harder. After a short wait she appeared in the kitchen, looking confused. "Have you got the wrong house?" she asked, smoothing her long black hair into place as she pushed open the door for him.

"I don't think so."

She made a face. "Your sneakers are wet. Look at the kitchen floor."

He looked at the wet tracks he was making on the linoleum. Then in a quick easy motion he flipped himself up and stood on his hands. "This better?" He began crossing the floor on his hands.

She laughed loudly. "That's great!" she said, following along behind him. "You're a real chimp. Can you eat with your feet?"

He tumbled over when he reached the hallway and

rolled to his feet. "Your turn," he said, gesturing to the floor.

"No way," she said, backing away. "Want a banana?"

He shook his head and plopped down on one of the overstuffed living room armchairs. He suddenly felt exhausted.

"Come in the den," she said, pulling his arm. "I don't want you on the good furniture. What are you doing here, anyway?"

"I don't know. Wrong house, I guess," he said.

She laughed again as she dragged him toward the den. He liked her laugh, he decided. It came from so deep in her throat. It was a sexy laugh. She looked cute, he thought. She was wearing faded jeans and an old Shadyside High sweatshirt with the collar ripped and frayed.

She pulled him harder, and he bumped into her. Her hair smelled of coconut. She must have shampooed it earlier. He inhaled deeply. He loved that smell.

"How's it going with you?" she asked. "Any better?"

"Better than what?" he asked, shoving some newspapers aside so he could drop down onto the black leather couch. "Better than being hit by a truck? Almost."

"That bad, huh?" she said sympathetically. She sat down beside him, her knee touching his leg.

"If I could just get my timing back on the rings." How many times had he said that lately?

"You'll get it back," she said, putting a hand comfortingly on his shoulder.

"Anna was waiting for me outside school," he said. "That was a surprise."

She removed her hand from his shoulder and sighed. "What did she want—some tips on how to do a hand-stand?"

He didn't notice her sarcasm. Seeing an article that interested him, he picked up the front section of the newspaper he had shoved aside. A car had spun out of control on Fear Street and crashed into a tree. The confused driver had no explanation for what had happened. The road was dry, and he had been traveling at a very slow speed.

"I love these visits of yours, Cory." Lisa's voice broke into his reading. "You tell me about Anna and then read the paper. You're a fun guy."

Cory put down the newspaper and started to apologize when the phone rang. "Who would call this late?" Lisa asked. She dived off the couch and got to the phone before it could ring a second time and wake her parents. "Hello?"

There was silence at the other end.

"Hello?" she repeated.

"You're dead too," a voice whispered in her ear. "You're dead too. You're dead too."

Just like on the note tied to the cat.

chapter

17

"*I*t was Anna who threatened me, Cory. She killed the cat. She made the threatening phone call."

"No, that's impossible," he insisted. "Come on, Lisa. Let's just dance and not talk about it." Cory pulled her toward the middle of the gym floor, where several other couples were already dancing. The floor vibrated to the music, a Missy Elliott album with a driving, machinelike drumbeat and pulsating bass that nearly drowned out the singer's voice.

Lisa made a halfhearted attempt to dance with Cory, but after a minute or two she stopped and pulled him back to the side. "You're just trying to change the subject," she said, holding on to his hands. Hers were cold despite the heat of the gym.

"No, I'm just trying to dance," he said, exasperated. "Why'd you ask me to this dance? If all you wanted to do was talk about Anna, we could have gone to my house, or your house."

"But she threatened my life, and all you do is defend her."

"It wasn't Anna," Cory said. "I know it. When I told Anna about the dead cat in your locker, she was horrified. Really. She felt terrible about it."

"So. She's a good actress," Lisa said, sneering. "Good enough to fool you."

A couple of guys from the gymnastics team waved at Cory from across the gym. He waved back. He wanted to run across the floor and talk to them. Kid around with them. Have some fun. This first date with Lisa was not working out.

"Why would Anna put a dead cat in your locker? Why? Why would she call and threaten you?" Cory asked, shouting over the music, a new album by Kanye West that was extremely difficult to shout over. "She doesn't even know you."

"She's jealous," Lisa said. "I told you."

"Get real," Cory told her, shaking his head in disbelief. He turned and started to walk away, but she followed right behind him. "Did she ask you to this dance?"

"Maybe."

"Come on—did she? Tell the truth."

"Well . . . yes."

"And was she standing in the hall spying on us when I asked you to this dance?"

"No. She wasn't spying. She—"

"She was listening, right? She was there in the hall.

124

She saw us together. And then afterward I got the dead cat with the note."

"That doesn't prove anything."

"Boy, are you loyal—to her!" Lisa snapped, her dark eyes filled with anger. Some kids standing nearby were staring at the two of them, startled to see what was obviously a heated argument grow even more heated.

Cory was embarrassed. "Lisa, please." He took her arm, but she pulled it away from him. "I know Anna. She wouldn't—"

"How well do you know Anna?" Lisa demanded. "How well?"

"It's got to be someone else who's trying to scare you. Someone who knows you."

"Who then? Who is it?"

"I don't know, but it isn't Anna!" Cory shouted. "Anna has her own problems. She doesn't have time to be making up problems for you."

"Oh, doesn't she?" Lisa's anger was getting the better of her. She shoved Cory hard in the chest, pushing him backward against the crepe paper streamers that lined the gym wall. "Come on and sit down. Maybe you'd like to tell me all about Anna's problems. Maybe we could spend all night discussing Anna's problems. You'd like that, wouldn't you?"

"Calm down, Lisa. Everyone's watching us."

"What *are* Anna's problems, Cory? Come on. Let's discuss them. What are her problems? Is she too thin? Is that her problem? Is she too pretty? That's it. I've guessed it, haven't I! She's too pretty, poor thing."

"Lisa—please. You're getting crazy over nothing."

"Nothing? Over nothing? Someone threatened my life. I guess that's nothing!"

"That's not what I meant, and you know it. Come on. Don't lose your temper. Let's dance or something. I apologize. Okay?"

"Apologize for what?"

"I don't know. For whatever."

She sighed and shook her head. "I should've known this wouldn't work out." The record had stopped. Her voice seemed to echo through the whole crowded gym. "You're just totally obsessed with that girl. Oh. I'm embarrassing you, aren't I, Cory?" Another record started.

"No. I mean, yes. I mean—"

"So sorry. I won't embarrass you anymore." She turned away from him and ran across the crowded dance floor. He started after her, then decided not to follow her. He watched her push her way through dancing couples until she made her way to the other side of the gym and disappeared through the double doors.

Now what?

Give her a little time to cool down and then go apologize to her? That was probably the best idea. He'd seen Lisa lose her temper hundreds of times before. She always flared up like a fire just taking hold, but her anger always faded as quickly as it came on.

Lisa was the jealous one, he decided. The idea made him smile despite the fight they had just had. She was jealous of Anna. And, of course, she had good reason to be.

Anna. For a split second he thought he saw her across the dance floor.

No, it couldn't be. He pushed her from his mind. He decided to go over to the refreshment table and get a Coke, maybe shoot the breeze with some guys for a while, and then go apologize to Lisa.

He was halfway across the gym when he heard the scream.

It was a girl's scream. A scream of terror.

The music stopped. Everyone heard it.

Cory knew at once.

It was Lisa's scream!

chapter

18

Several kids were already out in the dark corridor by the time Cory got there. A single amber bulb at the far end of the hall provided the only source of light. The kids were shadows, moving and shifting in the dark as they searched for the girl who had screamed. "There's no one here!" someone yelled, his voice echoing off the tile walls.

"Then, who screamed?" someone else asked.

Cory knew who had screamed. But where was she?

"I'm down here! Can somebody help me?" Lisa's voice floated up from the stairwell.

Taking them two at a time, Cory was the first one down the stairs.

"What's going on?"

"Who is it?"

"Is someone down there?"

Voices bounced around the empty hallways.

"Lisa—are you okay?" Cory asked. She was sitting on the floor at the bottom of the stairs.

"No, I don't think so."

He helped her to her feet, but she couldn't stand on her right foot. So he eased her back to the floor.

Several kids were on the stairway now, looking down at them in the dim light. "What happened?" "It's Lisa Blume." "Is she okay?" "Did she fall?"

"I—I'm okay," Lisa called up to them. "Sorry if I scared you. You can go back into the gym now. Really. I'll be okay."

A few kids lingered on the steps. Some guys started whistling loudly, seeing how it sounded in the echoing hallways. Eventually the music started in the gym again, and everyone went back inside.

"It's my ankle," Lisa told Cory, wincing with pain as she tried to stand on it again. "It got twisted. But I think it's okay. I just have to walk it off—if I can walk. Wow, I was lucky. I could've been killed. These stairs are *hard!*"

He let her lean her weight against him as she tested the ankle. "Did you fall?" he asked.

"No. I was pushed."

"What?"

"You heard me."

"But who—"

"Ouch!" she cried, and leaned harder on his arm. "How should I know? It was so dark. I was walking past the stairway. I didn't see anyone. I thought I was alone. It was so quiet out here, it was creepy. Just the sound of the drums vibrating from the gym. I—I think I'd better sit down."

He half carried her back onto the bottom step, where she dropped down heavily, breathing hard from the pain. "Hey—this is some memorable first date, huh?" she asked.

They both laughed, more from tension than from her remark. "So go on," Cory said. "What happened?"

"I don't know. I guess someone was there the whole time. I didn't hear footsteps or anything. Of course, I wasn't paying much attention. I was just concentrating on how mad I was at you."

"Thanks a bunch," Cory said sarcastically. "I knew this had to be my fault."

"Well, of course it is," she said, pulling him down beside her and holding on to his arm. "Suddenly two hands shoved me hard from behind. I saw this guy standing there as I fell down the stairs. I guess I screamed."

"Guy? What guy?"

"He was weird-looking. I couldn't see too well in the dark. He had watery eyes and sort of a puffy face. And he had a shiny earring in one ear."

"An earring?"

Cory's heart dropped to his knees.

"Brad!" he cried.

"Brad? Who's Brad? You know him?"

"He's Anna's brother," Cory said. "He's very crazy."

"But—he tried to kill me!" Lisa cried, starting to realize just what a close call she'd had. "Why would Anna's brother try to kill me?"

"I just thought of something," Cory said, jumping

to his feet. "Did the door open after you fell down the stairs?"

"What do you mean?" Lisa seemed confused.

"Did the outside door open? Did the guy with the earring run out?"

"No. I—I don't think so. No. I'm sure. The door never opened."

"Well, they keep all the other doors locked at night," Cory said excitedly. "Only the door near the gym is open for the dance. That means—"

"The person who pushed me is still in the building?"

"That's right. Let's take a little look around." He lifted her up off the step. "Can you walk?"

She put her foot down on the floor and tested it. "Yes. It's a little better."

He helped her up the stairs. "We'll search the long corridor first. Then we'll double back and search the shorter one." He was whispering now.

She leaned lightly against him, staying close as they walked. Their shoes clicked against the hard floor, the only sound in the long, dark corridor. "This is silly," she whispered.

"Maybe. Maybe not," Cory whispered back, his eyes straight ahead of him. "Shhhh." He stopped and held her back. He'd heard a noise in the language lab.

Was someone hiding in there?

They crept up to the glass-paneled door, which was pulled open about a third of the way, and listened. They heard it again. A shuffling sound, like the footsteps of someone scampering to a new hiding place.

They stood listening at the door for a few seconds. "Someone's in there," Cory whispered. "I think we're about to find the guy who pushed you."

He pulled the door open the rest of the way. The two of them stepped quickly into the large room. Lisa felt along the wall until she found the light switch, and turned on the lights.

"Who's in here?" Cory called.

The sound again.

They followed it across the room. One of the windows had been left open a few inches. The sound they'd been hearing was the venetian blind blowing in the wind.

"Good work, Sherlock," Lisa cracked, shaking her head. "You've caught the venetian blind in the act!"

Cory didn't laugh. "Come on. Let's keep searching," he said, turning off the lights. "If Brad is still in the building, I want to find him."

They turned the corner near Mr. Cardoza's classroom and walked on silently, Lisa leaning a little harder on Cory as her ankle began to swell and grow more painful. The hall grew darker as they walked away from the light.

Scratchy sounds. They both gasped. Something scampered in front of them, ducking into one of the classrooms. "What was that?" Lisa asked.

"Stop pulling on my sweater so hard. You're taking all the wool off," Cory complained.

"But what was that?" Lisa whispered loudly, gripping his arm even tighter.

"A four-legged creature," he said. "Probably a rat."

"Oh," she said. "Think there are more of them?"

"Probably."

They walked to the end of the corridor, sticking close together, then headed back, opening doors and peering into the dark, silent rooms. Nothing seemed the same. In the dark the familiar classrooms looked so much larger. They became mysterious caverns filled with creaking sounds and shifting shadows.

"Cory, I think you'd better take me home," Lisa whispered, sounding very discouraged. "Look at my ankle. It's about the size of a cantaloupe. I don't think I can walk much farther."

"Sure you don't want to dance some more?" It was Cory's feeble idea of a joke. They both knew it was feeble, but they laughed anyway.

But the laughter was cut short when they heard a voice coming from Mr. Burnette's biology classroom.

A young man's voice.

Very quiet. But definitely a young man's voice.

Lisa leaned against the cool tile wall for support. They crept silently to the doorway, which was open just a crack.

Another sound. A cough.

Someone was hiding in there.

"Brad?" Lisa whispered, putting her mouth right up to Cory's ear.

"We'll soon see," Cory whispered back, his heart pounding.

He pulled open the door and stepped inside.

He flicked on the light.

A girl screamed.

She was sitting on a boy's lap. Her lipstick was smeared across her chin.

Cory recognized the boy—Gary Harwood, a senior, a guy from the wrestling team.

"Hey, Brooks—what do you think you're doing?" Gary barked, squinting at the sudden light.

"Give us a break," the girl said, frowning, her arm still around Gary's massive shoulder. "Can't we have some privacy?"

"Yeah. Get lost," Gary said menacingly.

"Sorry," Cory managed to say. He carefully turned off the lights and backed out of the room.

Lisa was already in the hall, leaning against the wall, laughing and shaking her head. Cory reached out and pulled her hair. "Not funny," he insisted.

She pulled him across the hall into the small music room. She was laughing so hard, tears rolled down her cheeks.

"Don't get hysterical on me," he said, forcing a straight face.

"But it is hysterical," she said, wiping her cheeks with her open hands. "A guy from the wrestling team. That's who you pick on? He'll murder you! He cracks walnuts against his neck!" She started laughing all over again.

"It's not funny," Cory insisted. "Come on. We've got to keep searching. If the guy who pushed you is still—"

He stopped in mid-sentence. Someone had stepped into the shadows of the doorway. First Cory saw the sleeve of the black fur parka as the dark figure grabbed

134

the doorknob. Then he saw the hood pulled up to shield the man's face.

Lisa grabbed Cory's arm. "That—that's *him*," she whispered.

The hood slid back as the man entered the room.

It was Brad.

chapter

19

*B*rad stepped back into darkness. But they had already seen his face.

Surprisingly, he looked more frightened than they did.

He started toward them, pulling the parka hood back up over his head as if he could hide inside it. Cory and Lisa stepped back toward the tall windows. Lisa backed into a music stand, sending it toppling to the floor. The loud crash made them both cry out, startled.

Brad stopped halfway into the room.

His eyes were darting from side to side. He seemed unable to decide what to do next. He muttered something under his breath. Cory could hear only the last word: "Mistake."

Brad said it again. Again Cory could hear only "mistake."

Was Brad threatening them? Was he warning them

not to come after him? They couldn't tell. They couldn't hear him.

Brad stood staring at them, his tiny black eyes wide in panic. Inside the parka his forehead was covered with large beads of perspiration. His face was bright red.

Suddenly he turned and, without saying another word, fled from the room. Cory pulled away from Lisa's frightened grip and ran after him.

But Brad slammed the door hard before Cory could get there. And then Cory and Lisa heard a loud bang.

"Hey!" Lisa yelled.

Cory tried the knob. He tried it again. Again. He tried pulling. Then pushing. He turned to her, looking very worried. "It won't turn. He must have shoved something against the door."

"Are you sure? Maybe you're pushing when you should be pulling."

"You want to try it?" Cory snapped.

She slumped down on a folding chair and gently rubbed her ankle. "No. Guess I'll take your word for it. Was that Anna's brother?"

"Yeah."

"Are we gonna call the police when we get out of here? *If* we get out of here," she added, just to show that she could still be her usual sarcastic self.

"I don't know," Cory said, trying the door again without success. "I—I think I'd like to talk to Anna first. She might be in danger. If we send the police after Brad, there's no telling what he might do to Anna."

"Let's just get out of here," Lisa said wearily.

"How are we—oh, I know. Call Harwood. He and that girl are probably still making out across the hall, right?"

Cory shrugged. He put his face against the door and yelled, "Hey—Harwood—let us out of here! *Harwood!*"

No response.

He tried again, louder. Still no reply.

"Oh, how stupid!" Lisa said. "Stop yelling. No one can hear. This is the music room. Everything is sound-proof."

Cory stood staring at the doorknob for a few seconds. Then he turned, ran to the window, and pulled up the metal blinds. The room looked down on the student parking lot. It was a clear night. The rows of cars reflected the bright parking lot pole lights.

"Hey—look!" Cory yelled.

Brad was running to a small car on the edge of the lot. Cory watched him climb into the car and speed away, his tires squealing on the asphalt.

"Come on—let's get out of here," Cory said. He unlocked one of the windows and pulled it all the way open.

"But we're two stories up," Lisa protested.

Cory stuck his head out the window and leaned way out. A few seconds later he pulled it back in. "No problem," he said, grinning. "I'm a gymnast, remember?"

"Uh-oh. I don't like that smile on your face. Are you going into your Tarzan act now?"

"Yeah," he said, scratching himself and nodding his head like Tarzan's chimp.

"Well, I don't exactly feel like Jane," Lisa said, wincing in pain as she tried to put weight on her ankle.

"No problem. I'll come back for you," Cory said.

"What are you going to do?"

"There's a three-inch ledge that runs under the windows. I'm going to walk the ledge to that sycamore tree, then climb onto that extending branch, then slide down the trunk."

"Maybe we should just stay here until they open school Monday morning," Lisa said.

"Thanks for the encouragement," Cory said, looking down at the narrow granite ledge.

"We could sit back, relax, and watch my ankle swell," Lisa suggested, hobbling over to the window, taking Cory's hand and pulling him back from the window.

"No problem," Cory told her, pulling away. He lifted a leg over the window and started to ease himself out onto the ledge. "Really. No problem. I could do this blindfolded."

Lisa moved away from the window, plopped down into a chair, and put her ankle up on the attached desk. She couldn't bear to watch.

Cory had both feet on the ledge now. He was still holding on to the bottom of the window frame. He looked to his left. He had to move only ten feet or so and then he would be at the tree.

He carefully turned around so that he was facing the window. He took a sideways step. "Hey! It's slippery!"

"Oh, great!" Lisa called, rubbing her sore ankle. "Get back in here!"

"No. I'm outta here," he said, but he didn't sound quite as confident as he had a few seconds before.

He had to let go of the window frame to take a second step. That meant he was now pressing against solid brick.

Moving slowly, carefully, his palms pressed against the brick wall, he took another sideways step. Then another.

To his dismay the ledge suddenly narrowed. He had to stand on tiptoe to stay on it. But standing on tiptoe made it harder to balance.

He realized he'd been holding his breath the whole time. He exhaled and took a deep breath. He turned his head and looked back over his shoulder at the tree.

The tree seemed farther away than it had from inside the building. And as he edged closer, he realized that the branch he planned to climb on to wasn't as close to the ledge as it had originally appeared. In fact, it was at least four feet away, maybe farther.

He was just realizing that he'd never be able to reach the tree branch when his right foot slid off the slippery ledge and he started to fall.

chapter

20

Using his gymnastics reflexes, Cory reached up as he started to drop and grabbed the ledge as he would a parallel bar.

He missed.

His hands slid off the wet stone ledge and he continued to drop, his body sliding straight down against the brick wall.

"Hey!" His feet hit a ledge on the first floor, and instinctively he dived forward, falling through an open window. He landed hard on his hands and knees on a wood floor.

It took him what seemed forever to catch his breath. Then he slowly got up on his knees and looked around the dark room. He recognized it immediately. He had fallen into the woodshop. "I'll have to thank whoever left that window open," he said aloud.

He stood up and stretched, and tested his body. He seemed okay except that he still had the feeling he was falling. Remembering Lisa, he hurried out of the shop and into the hallway. He could hear the drum rhythms from the music in the gym echoing down the tiled corridor. He turned and took the steps two at a time, and ran to the music room. He saw the hall monitor's desk had been jammed against the door. It was heavy, but he shoved it aside and opened the door to the music room. "That was quick," Lisa said. She was still slumping in the chair with her ankle up on the desk.

"I took a shortcut," he said.

A half hour later they were sitting on the low couch in her living room. Lisa propped her swollen ankle up on the coffee table and settled back comfortably against the cushions.

"Some adventure," Cory said dejectedly. He was thinking about Brad. And Anna. Poor Anna.

"Some first date," she said, staring straight ahead at her ankle. "I'm really sorry. I—"

"No. I'm sorry," he said.

She leaned forward suddenly and started to kiss him, a soft, tentative kiss.

The phone beside the couch rang. They both jumped back.

She picked it up quickly, pushing her hair away from her face with her free hand. "Hello?"

She heard breathing at the other end.

"Hello? Hello?"

"Who is it?" Cory asked her.

She shrugged. "Hello?"

More breathing. Harsh, rhythmic breathing. Meant to sound threatening.

"Why are you doing this to me?" Lisa cried.

The phone went dead.

Lisa tossed down the receiver. Her hands were shaking, but she looked more angry than frightened. "This has got to stop!" she cried.

Cory moved across the couch, intending to comfort her. But she pulled away from him. "We've got to call the police," Lisa said.

"I know. I know," Cory agreed. "Just let me talk to Anna first. I'll go see her first thing in the morning."

"But Brad will be there, won't he?"

"I don't care. I'm not afraid of Brad. I'll get to Anna. And I'll make Anna tell me what's going on. And I'll tell Anna that we have no choice. We have to report Brad to the police."

"Ouch!" She dropped back down to the couch and started rubbing her ankle. "Hey, some date. I really know how to show a guy a good time, don't I?"

"At least it wasn't boring!" he said, forcing a laugh. He got up and started for the door. "Sure you'll be okay?"

"Yeah. Sure. Call me right after you talk to her tomorrow, you hear?"

"Right. Don't worry."

"Good luck tomorrow."

"Thanks," he said. "I'll need it."

chapter
21

*H*e turned the car onto Fear Street,
cruised the long block, and this time pulled right up
the gravel drive to the Corwin house. He had never
seen the house in daylight. It looked even shabbier
with a bright sun beaming down on its faded shingles
and falling gutters.

His parents had wondered where he was going so
early on a Sunday morning. He had told them he had
a special gymnastics team workout. He didn't like
lying to them, especially when it was such a feeble lie.
But he couldn't very well tell them he was driving to
Fear Street to find out why a girl's brother was terror-
izing him and Lisa and had tried to kill Lisa.

He didn't really know what he'd do if Brad answered
the door. He'd been up most of the night thinking
about it but hadn't been able to come up with a plan.
All night he had tried to sort out his feelings about
Anna. He felt angry at himself for becoming involved

with her and her sick, crazy brother. Yet he also felt sorry for her. And he was frightened for her. And . . . and . . . he was still terribly attracted to her, to her old-fashioned prettiness, to her teasing sexiness, to her . . . differentness.

All these weeks he had spent thinking of nothing but Anna. And still, to this very moment, she was a complete mystery to him.

Well, no more.

He was about to unravel the mystery. All of the mysteries. He wasn't going to leave until his every question was answered.

He knocked loudly on the door.

No response. He waited awhile.

Ignoring the pounding in his chest and the impulse to run as far from this house as he could, he raised his fist and pounded again.

Silence.

He knocked again, harder. Then again.

He waited. There wasn't a sound inside the house, no sign that anyone was there.

More angry than disappointed, Cory turned and started back to the car.

"Morning."

It was the strange neighbor. He was leaning on the hood of Cory's car. He was wearing the same rain slicker and white tennis hat, even though it was a bright, sunny morning. Voltaire, the big Doberman, was at his side. Cory jumped back, then was relieved to see that the dog was on a leash.

"Don't ever see you much in the daytime," the man said, grinning at Cory, not exactly a friendly grin, but a more pleasant expression than Cory had ever seen on him.

"Guess not," Cory said, walking slowly to the car.

"They're not home," the man said, pointing to the house. "Left early this morning."

"Oh," Cory said. "Know where they went?"

The man seemed offended by the question. "I'm no snoop," he said curtly.

"You seem to know a lot about them," Cory said.

The man looked at him thoughtfully. "Can't help but notice some things when you're a neighbor," he said finally. "You seem like an all-right young man."

The compliment startled Cory. "Thanks."

"That's why I can't understand your comin' to visit them," he said pointedly. The dog barked. "Okay, okay, Voltaire." The man pulled himself up from Cory's car. "Be seein' you," he said, giving Cory a wave as if they were old friends, and then trotted off to keep up with his pulling dog.

"Not if I see you first," Cory said under his breath. Neither the old guy nor his dog seemed as threatening in the daytime, though. Just a snoopy neighbor out walking his dog day and night, trying to see what he can learn around the neighborhood.

Well, Cory had learned absolutely nothing. He took one last look at the old house, then dejectedly got back into the car. He had spent the whole night going over and over what he was going to say. And now there was no one to say any of it to.

He spent the afternoon trying to do some homework. He was terribly behind. He called the Corwins' house every half hour. There was no one home all day or all evening.

The next morning, feeling nervous and out-of-sorts, he drove to school early and waited by Anna's locker for her to show up. But she hadn't arrived when the bell rang, and he went to his homeroom, disappointed again.

He didn't catch up with her until after school. Then he ran into her by accident outside the biology lab.

She looked for a moment as if she didn't recognize him. Then her expression changed and she gave him a warm smile. "Cory. Hi."

"I—I've got to talk to you."

"I can't. I've got to go home and—"

He grabbed her arm. He wasn't sure why. He wasn't sure what he planned to do. He just knew he wasn't going to let her get away. "No. You're coming with me. I've got to talk to you. I'll take you home after."

She didn't resist. She could see that he was serious, that he wouldn't take no for an answer.

He led her to his car in silence, pulling her as if she were a captive, not letting go of her hand, as if she might slip away and disappear into thin air if he didn't hold on. He drove to the Division Street Mall. She played with the radio, pushing the buttons in order, listening to a station for ten seconds, then moving on to the next.

At the Pizza Oven he guided her to a booth in the back. She slid in across from him, smiling uneasily, her eyes darting nervously to the front of the long, narrow restaurant. It was quiet. Only a few booths were filled. Most of the after-school crowd hadn't arrived yet.

A waitress slouched over to them, cracking her bubble gum noisily. Cory ordered two Cokes. Then he turned to Anna and took her hand. "Tell me the truth about you, and about Brad," he said, staring into her deep blue, mysteriously opaque eyes. "I want to know what's going on. Everything."

She didn't question him. She seemed to know that she had no choice this time. And once she started talking, she seemed eager to get the story out, desperate to tell it to him, relieved to finally have someone to tell it to.

"I moved here last month with my mother and Brad," she began, looking at Cory, then shifting her gaze to the front window of the restaurant, then back to Cory. "My father left us, just disappeared several years ago. My mother is not well. She's very frail. Brad has always been the head of the family.

"About a year ago," she continued, talking rapidly in her soft voice, "something terrible happened to Brad. He was in love with a girl named Emily. Emily was killed in a plane crash. It was just awful. And Brad never recovered from the shock."

"What do you mean?" Cory asked.

"He lost his grip on reality. He just couldn't take Emily's death. For a while he imagined that Emily was still alive. We had a sister. Her name was Willa. Willa was a year older than me. She looked like me, but she was really beautiful. She was the true beauty of the family.

"After Emily died, Brad got very protective of Willa

and me. He got very crazy, very mixed up. He started calling Willa by the wrong name. He started calling her Emily. Soon after that he started telling people that Willa was dead—even when she was standing right there in the room!

"We didn't know what to do with Brad. He was so mixed up. We tried to get him to go to a doctor. But he refused."

"Here's the Cokes. Pay now, please," the waitress interrupted.

Cory pulled out his wallet and found two dollar bills. Anna tore the paper off the straw and greedily drank her Coke almost to the bottom without taking a breath.

"Go on. Please," Cory urged.

"The story just gets worse," she said. A single large tear formed in each eye. Her eyes look like two blue lakes, Cory thought.

"Brad kept confusing Willa and Emily. He kept saying Willa was dead. Then, one horrible day, it happened. Willa was killed. She fell down the basement stairs."

Cory groaned aloud. "How awful—"

"Brad was home at the time. He said it was an accident. Willa was carrying some clothes down to the basement, and she just slipped and fell. But Mom and I never believed him. We suspected that Brad had pushed Willa.

"First, you see, he was telling people that Willa was dead. And then—she really *was* dead!

"We were so frightened. We were terrified of Brad, of what he might do next. But we had no one else to support us. Dad left when we were little. He just took off. Mom was too sick to work and too proud to take welfare. We had no one but Brad. So what could we do? We *had* to believe his story that Willa's death was an accident.''

"So then you moved to Shadyside?" Cory asked.

"No. Not yet. This was still last spring. Brad seemed better for a while. But then his mind became confused again. He started telling people that *I* was dead. I was so scared, I didn't know what to do. Was Brad going to kill me next? I was terrified every day.''

"I don't believe this. I just don't believe it,'' Cory said, offering her his Coke since she had finished hers.

She took a long sip. "Somehow Mom got the strength to insist that we move. We moved here to Shadyside. We hoped the new surroundings would help snap Brad out of his shock, his confusion. But it hasn't helped. He keeps telling people that I'm dead. And at the same time he's terribly overprotective. He won't let me go out, or have dates, or anything. Some days he won't even let me go to school.''

"So that explains it,'' Cory said, more to himself than to her. The dreadful details of her story were still spinning through his mind. This poor girl is living in a nightmare, he thought. I've got to find a way to help her. We've got to get Brad out of the house.

But then he remembered something.

"Hey, wait a minute,'' he said.

"What?'' She looked as if she were dreading what he was about to say.

"I saw a newspaper clipping. From Melrose. It said that you were dead. It had a picture and everything.''

"Oh." She flushed. Her hands gripped the edge of the Formica tabletop. She was thinking hard. She didn't seem to have an answer. "Oh, yes. I remember that newspaper thing now," she said, her normal color returning. "I guess I blocked it. Isn't it horrible? Can you imagine seeing your own obituary in the newspaper? Brad claimed that the newspaper got it all wrong. But I think Brad just couldn't face Willa's death, and so he told them it was me."

Cory shook his head in disbelief.

"Cory, I'm so frightened all the time," Anna said, grabbing his hand in hers. "I don't know what to think. Is Brad confusing me with Emily? Is he confusing me with Willa? Since he's telling people I'm dead, does it mean he plans to kill me too? I'm really scared—especially now that my mother is visiting her sister. . . . Brad and I are alone. . . ."

Cory just stared back at her, at the soft tears forming along the rims of her beautiful eyes, at her golden hair. He didn't know what to say. It was such a sad and frightening story.

Suddenly she leaned across the tabletop and pulled his face close to hers. She began to kiss him, gently at first and then harder.

Then, just as suddenly, she stopped and pulled back.

Her face filled with horror.

Cory turned around in the booth to see what she was looking at. There was Brad outside the front window, his face pressed to the glass, a look of fury on his face.

"I—I've got to go," Anna said, her face filled with panic.

She leapt up from the booth and disappeared out the back door of the restaurant.

Cory turned to the front. Brad hadn't moved from the window. He was staring straight ahead at Cory, his face frozen in hatred, in rage.

chapter
22

*H*e tried to call Lisa as soon as he got home, but she was out with her family. Then, after dinner, he tried to call Anna. The phone rang and rang. He let it ring twenty times. He counted the rings.

Then, his head spinning with frightening images, images of Brad's furious face, images of Anna's fear, images of Anna falling down endless basement stairs, he hung up.

He tried five minutes later, and five minutes after that, letting the phone ring twenty times each call, but with the same results.

What if something had happened to her? What if Brad, in his rage at seeing them together in the restaurant, had done something to her?

No. He couldn't allow himself to think that.

But he had to. Brad had already killed once. Or so

Anna believed. Who was to say that he couldn't kill again?

Standing with his red face pressed against the restaurant window, his eyes bugging out, his mouth twisted in fury, Brad had certainly looked like someone who could kill.

Cory picked up the phone and, ignoring his trembling hand, dialed the Corwin house again. Someone picked up on the sixth ring.

"Yeah?"

Cory recognized the harsh voice. "Brad? I know Anna's there. Put her on the phone."

"Anna isn't anywhere. Anna is dead."

The phone clicked off. Brad had hung up on him.

What did Brad mean? Was Anna really dead now? Had Brad just killed her?

No. This was just another of Brad's sick, twisted fantasies.

Or was it?

Cory realized he had no choice. He pulled on his jacket, ran down the stairs two at a time, and grabbed the car keys from the front entranceway table. "Hey—where are you going?" his mom called.

He mumbled an answer. He wasn't sure what he said. He pulled the front door closed behind him, and a few seconds later he was speeding through a thick, wet fog, driving blindly, with Anna's face his only guidepost, driving once again to Fear Street.

"Anna, be alive," he said to himself. "Please—be alive, be alive, be alive." The windshield wipers, clearing the wet fog from the glass, clicked the rhythm to his words: "Be alive, be alive, be alive . . . ."

The drive seemed to take hours. Finally he pulled up the long gravel drive to the Corwin house and squealed to a stop. Not turning off the engine or the lights, he threw open the car door and ran up to the porch.

He stopped at the front door, raised his hand, and knocked—and heard a loud scream.

A scream of anger, of fury.

"He's come for me! Let me go!!"

She's alive, he thought.

And without hesitating he pushed open the heavy wooden front door and burst into the house. He found himself in a dark, narrow entranceway with a small coat closet along the wall. He inhaled the powerful smell of mothballs. Beyond the entranceway was the living room, lighted only by a small, flickering fire in the fireplace.

"Let me go!" he heard Anna scream. "He's come to see me! Me!"

His heart pounding, Cory ran into the living room. There on the floor in front of the fireplace, Anna and Brad appeared to be locked in a desperate fight. She was sitting on his chest, struggling to remove his arms from around her waist so that she could stand up. She managed to pin his arms down, but Brad reached up a hand and pushed under her chin until her head snapped back. Then he quickly rolled out from under her and gave her a hard shove that sent her sprawling toward the fire. With a loud groan he climbed to his feet, prepared to attack again.

Cory hurtled across the room, his arms outstretched, ready to help Anna any way he could.

Hearing Cory approach, Brad turned around, startled. But he turned too late. Cory leapt onto his back. Cory drove a fist into Brad's side, and both of them fell to the floor and began wrestling to get the advantage.

"Cory! You're here!" Anna cried, recovering and moving away from the fire.

Brad swung around, trying to land a punch in Cory's midsection. But Cory scrambled away and the punch went wild.

"Get out of here!" Brad shouted, saliva dripping down his chin, his small eyes wild with rage. "You don't know what you're doing! You don't want to be here!"

"Too late!" Cory cried. He lowered his head and rammed it into Brad's chest. Brad cried out and staggered backward.

"Help me, Cory! Please—help me!" Anna was shrieking from the corner of the room. She was holding her hands over her ears as if trying to shut out a deafening sound.

But Cory and Brad were scuffling in silence now.

Brad was soft and not very powerful, but he was bigger than Cory and seemed to be more experienced at fighting. He spun Cory around and shoved him hard into the wall.

Dazed, Cory dropped to all fours and tried to shake it off. But Brad leapt quickly onto his back and began pulling his head back.

"My neck! You're going to break my neck!" Cory screamed.

But his cries made Brad pull back even harder.

"Help me, Cory. Help me!" Anna continued to scream, wedging herself tightly in the corner of the room.

Still pulling Cory's head back, Brad lifted Cory to his feet. Cory struggled to breathe. He realized he was about to go under, about to lose consciousness. The pain made it so hard to move, so hard to think.

Somehow he grabbed a vase off the table beside the couch. It was heavy and nearly slipped from his hand. But with one last burst of strength he brought the vase down hard over Brad's head.

Brad's eyes shut tightly from the pain. He uttered a short cry that faded as he dropped to the floor. Cory, gasping for air, took a step back, trying to ready himself for Brad's next onslaught. But it didn't come. Brad fell heavily onto the floor and didn't move. He was unconscious.

Before Cory could regain his balance, Anna was in his arms. She threw her arms around him, nearly knocking him over, and pressed her face against his. "Thank you," she whispered. "Thank you, thank you. I knew you would come. I knew it."

Cory's heart was pounding so hard, it felt about to explode. His chest heaved as he struggled to catch his breath. His muscles ached from the strain of the fight, and he began to feel sick to his stomach.

"I knew you would come. I knew it," Anna repeated, pressing against him.

"We—we've got to call the police," Cory said, trying to back away from her grasp, trying to calm himself, slow his breathing.

"Thank you for saving me. Thank you." Her breath was hot against his cheek.

He looked down at Brad, still sprawled unconscious on the carpet. "Anna—please. We've got to move quickly. Brad won't be out for long," Cory pleaded. He wasn't sure Anna was hearing him. "We've got to get you away from here. We've got to make sure you're safe from him."

"Yes," she whispered. "Yes." She took his hands and started to pull him toward the stairway in the front hall. "Come with me, Cory. We're alone now. He can't bother us." She kissed his cheek, his forehead. She gave him a devilish look. "Come to my room, Cory. He can't bother us now."

"No, Anna—please. We've got to call the police," he insisted. Her eyes were wild, unreal, like big blue buttons. Her face seemed to glow with excitement. "Anna—Brad will wake up soon. We can't—"

She pulled him up the creaking, uneven stairs. "We have to celebrate, Cory. You and me. Come." A sexy, inviting smile spread across her face. Her eyes grew even wider, even more opaque.

Cory gave in. He realized he couldn't resist her. He started to follow her up the stairs.

"I want to show you something, Cory," she said as they reached the landing.

"What? What is it, Anna?"

"This," she said. The smile faded instantly from her face. Her eyes narrowed. She reached down to a low table in the narrow hallway and picked something up in her hand.

What was it?

Cory had trouble making it out in the dimly lit hallway.

She held it up. It was a silver letter opener shaped like a dagger, sharp as a dagger, too, from the looks of it.

"Anna—" Cory felt the fear well up in his chest.

"This will take care of Brad," she said. She plunged it through the air, a practice swing.

"No!" Cory yelled. "I won't let you."

"I won't let anyone stand in my way," she said. "Not even you."

She raised the letter opener above her head. She moved toward him, brandishing it like a knife. In the shadowy light her face became hard, frightening, ugly with hate.

"Put that down!" he cried, backing up, confused, not sure this was really happening. Hadn't he just saved her? Wasn't she just in his arms thanking him, inviting him up to her room? "Anna, what are you doing? Stop. We have to call the police!"

Her eyes were clear and cold. She didn't respond, didn't seem to hear him. She swung the letter opener down fast, trying to stab him in the chest.

Cory leapt backward. The blade missed him by less than an inch.

She lunged forward, raising the blade again, preparing another attack. He backed up, raising his hands to fend her off. "Anna—what are you doing? Anna—please—listen to me!"

His back, he realized, was against an open window. He had no room to move now.

She moved quickly forward, thrusting the silver blade in front of her.

He tried to move back, dodge out of the way.

She lunged at him.

He tried to jump out of the way, lost his balance, and fell back—out the open window.

chapter

23

*I*t was as if it were happening in slow motion. First he felt his feet leave the floor. Then he saw the black sky and felt the shock of the cold night air on his face.

Then he knew he was falling, falling backward, falling down, headfirst.

Instinctively, his legs bent. He caught them around the windowsill. He was a gymnast, after all, he told himself. He had skills. He just had to use them.

He had to use them. Or die.

The backs of his knees hit the windowsill. He clamped his legs tightly and held on. Then he swung himself up, using the strong stomach muscles he had developed through years of practice. He flipped himself up until his head was upright, then slid easily back into the hallway.

Anna hadn't moved. She stood in the hallway, holding the letter opener in front of her, staring blankly at the window.

Cory did a forward flip across the hallway and kicked the letter opener from her hand.

She shrieked and seemed to come out of her shock. He landed on his feet and stared at her. Her face, which had been expressionless as she stared at the window, filled with anger. With a desperate cry, a wild animal cry of attack, she lunged at him.

Dodging to the side, he grabbed her as she moved past him. He spun her around and pulled her arms behind her back.

"Let me go! Let me go!" she screamed. But she was light and weak, no match for him.

He held her arms firmly behind her back and began to move forward, pushing her to the stairs. She struggled with all of her strength, shrieking and cursing him.

He started to pull her down the stairs when he heard a sound. Looking down, he saw to his horror that Brad had revived.

Brad was coming up the stairs after him.

Cory was trapped.

chapter
24

"*S*tay away, Brad. Stay away!" Cory heard himself shouting.

He wasn't making any sense. Why would Brad stay away?

"I warned you," Brad called up wearily. He was halfway up the stairs.

Anna struggled to free herself, but Cory held on tight. He looked back up to the open window. For a brief moment he considered dropping Anna or tossing her down at Brad, then leaping out the window.

"I tried to frighten you away," Brad said, climbing toward him slowly, deliberately. "I tried to scare you, to keep you from getting involved with her."

"Go away, Brad!" Anna screamed.

Brad took another step closer. Anna struggled. Cory tightened his grip.

"I just wanted to keep you safe from her," Brad said.

"Shut up, Brad! I'll kill you too!" Anna shrieked.

With a burst of strength she pulled out of Cory's grasp. She dived for the letter opener. But Cory caught her again and pulled her back.

Brad sat down on the top step and rubbed the back of his head. Cory suddenly realized that Brad had no intention of fighting him.

"Want to know the whole story?" Brad asked Cory. "You're not going to like it."

"Shut up, Brad! Shut up!" Anna cried.

"I've been telling you the truth. Anna is dead."

"Shut up shut up shut up!"

"She isn't Anna. She's Willa. She's Anna's sister."

Cory was so stunned, he nearly let her go.

"When Anna fell down the stairs and died, Mom and I suspected that it wasn't an accident, that Willa pushed her," Brad said, rubbing the bump on his head. "She was always insanely jealous of Anna. Anna had everything. Anna was beautiful. She had a million friends. She got straight A's without having to study hard. Willa couldn't compete in any way—and Anna never let her forget it."

"Shut up, Brad. I mean it—"

"But I couldn't prove that Willa had killed Anna. And Mom isn't well. I knew she couldn't survive losing both her daughters. So I never did anything about Willa.

"After Anna's so-called accident, Willa seemed to be okay," Brad continued, his voice soft and shaky, so soft Cory had to struggle to hear. "But I kept close watch over her. We moved here. I hoped the new surroundings would help us all forget the tragedy of losing Anna. It was a stupid thing to hope for."

"Shut up, Brad. You're stupid. You've always been stupid!" Willa shrieked, still struggling to free herself from Cory's grasp.

"Like I said, Willa actually seemed okay once we moved here," Brad told Cory, ignoring his sister's outburst. "At least, she acted perfectly normal at home. But when you started coming around, asking for Anna, I began to suspect what Willa was doing. I noticed that she started to dress like Anna. And talk like her. I tried to scare you away, Cory. I did my best to keep you from getting involved with her. I figured out that she was calling herself Anna at school, that she was trying to slip into Anna's identity."

"I'm going to kill you!" Willa shrieked, her eyes on the letter opener.

"I knew I should've gotten Willa professional help," Brad said sadly. "But we just couldn't afford it. I was foolish. I should've done something for Willa. Anything."

"I'm going to kill you too!" Willa screamed. "I'm going to kill you both!"

"I know she's been making phone calls to you and to that girl who's your friend. I know she's been making all kinds of threats, leading you on, forcing you to meet her, drawing you into her web. I guess she can't help herself."

"Wait just a minute," Cory broke in. "I have one little problem with your story, Brad. What about the other night at the dance? That wasn't Anna—I mean,

Willa—who pushed Lisa down the stairs. That was you.''

"I *told* you that was a mistake," Brad said heatedly. "I told you in the music room it was all a mistake. I followed Willa to the dance. I figured she was going there to make trouble for you. I wanted to stop her. I waited for her there in the hall. It was dark. I couldn't see much of anything. I thought it was Willa who was hurrying past me. I made a grab for her. I didn't really mean to push her, but she fell. Then when I got a good look at her, I realized I had grabbed the wrong girl. I watched to make sure she wasn't badly hurt. Then I panicked and hid. I didn't know what to do. I felt terrible about it. I was just trying to protect you from Willa."

"Anna went to the dance—not Willa. Willa is *dead!*" Willa broke in. "Stop calling me Willa. I'm not Willa. I'm Anna! I'm Anna! I'm Anna!" She began wailing at the top of her lungs.

Brad stood up and held out his arms. Cory handed Willa over to him. She slumped against Brad, exhausted.

"Call the police," Brad told Cory. "We've got to get her some help."

chapter

25

"*C*ory, you've eaten half a chocolate cake!"

"Don't worry. I'll save you a slice." He cut himself another large chunk and slid it onto his plate. He'd been starving ever since he'd left the Corwins' house.

Lisa sat down close to him on the leather den couch and watched him eat. "So that's the whole story?" she asked.

He swallowed a mouthful of icing. "Yeah. That's all of it," he said, suddenly no longer feeling hungry.

"And I was right. About the dead cat and the phone calls—it was all Anna."

"No. All Willa," he corrected her. "But yeah. You were right." He frowned and put the plate on the coffee table. "Another horror story from the folks on Fear Street," he said bitterly. He felt unsteady, shaky, as if he might burst out screaming—or crying. He stared at the wall, trying to get himself together. He was experiencing so many feelings at once, he couldn't sort them out.

She put a hand gently on his shoulder. "When it comes to girlfriends, you sure know how to pick 'em," she said.

He sighed. "Yeah. Maybe from now on I should let you pick them for me."

Her hand went up to his face. She rubbed the back of her hand tenderly over his cheek. "Maybe I should," she said softly.

He turned and looked at her. "Got anyone in mind?"

Their faces were inches apart. She moved forward to fill in the inches. She kissed him, a long kiss, a sweet kiss.

"Maybe . . ." she said.

About the Author

R.L. Stine invented the teen horror genre with Fear Street, the bestselling teen horror series of all time. He also changed the face of children's publishing with the mega-successful Goosebumps series, which *Guinness World Records* cites as the Best-Selling Children's Book Series ever, and went on to become a worldwide multimedia phenomenon. The first two books in his new series Mostly Ghostly, *Who Let the Ghosts Out?* and *Have You Met My Ghoulfriend?*, are *New York Times* bestsellers. He's thrilled to be writing for teens again in the brand-new Fear Street Nights books.

R.L. Stine has received numerous awards of recognition, including several Nickelodeon Kids' Choice Awards and Disney Adventures Kids' Choice Awards, and he has been selected by kids as one of their favorite authors in the National Education Association Read Across America. He lives in New York City with his wife, Jane, and their dog, Nadine.